OPTICS

OPTICS

LIGHT FOR A NEW AGE

JEFF HECHT

CHARLES SCRIBNER'S SONS • NEW YORK

For Jolyn and Leah

ACKNOWLEDGMENTS

Shirley Mishara, Don O'Shea, Marilyn Johnson, Mary Johnson, and Lois Hecht gave me valuable comments on earlier versions of some chapters. I made the drawings using an Apple Macintosh computer, MacDraw and laser printer, with help from Noel Gouveia. Clare Costello at Scribners gracefully tolerated my uncertainties and delays and helped convince me this book was possible. Thanks also to Irwin Math, Jarus Quinn, and my fellow members of the Optical Society of America's Education Council.

Charles Scribner's Sons Books for Young Readers
Macmillan Publishing Company, 866 Third Avenue, New York, NY 10022
Collier Macmillan Canada, Inc.

Printed in the United States of America
First Edition   10 9 8 7 6 5 4 3 2

Library of Congress Cataloging-in-Publication Data
Hecht, Jeff.   Optics : light for a new age.
Includes index.
Summary: Describes the wonders of light and optics, exploring
such developments as lasers, fiber optics, and holography.
1. Optics—Juvenile literature. [1. Optics. 2. Light] I. Title.
QC360.H43 1987   535   87-23398   ISBN 0-684-18879-1

CONTENTS

1

Optics and Light

Light is all around us. Without light, you could not see to read these words. Light from the sun heats the earth and provides the energy that plants need to grow. Light can carry messages or even perform surgery. It brings us beauty in sunsets, rainbows, and laser light shows.

Optics is the ancient and wonderful science of light. Human beings have always been fascinated by light and thousands of years ago thought mirrors and glass were magical. Throughout history, optical instruments have opened new doors. Since Galileo Galilei first turned a telescope to the heavens in 1610, light from distant planets, stars, and galaxies has taught us about the immense universe. We first learned about very small things later in the century, when Antony van Leeuwenhoek and others looked through microscopes to discover a world that people had never before seen.

Today we probe the universe with new telescopes that can see much farther than Galileo ever dreamed of. When the space shuttle is launched again, one of its first loads will be the Hubble space telescope. The largest telescope ever—ten meters (nearly forty feet) across—is being built in Hawaii. Microscopes have improved so much that any you use in your school gives a much clearer view than van Leeuwenhoek ever had.

New optical devices are making light for our age. The past thirty years have seen the coming of the laser and the optical fiber. With them, scientists and engineers have made breakthroughs in many fields. Today light can read, write, heal, cut, and do many other things. Tomorrow it will do even more.

In this book we will explore the wonders of light and optics and see how the old magic became the new science.

What Is Light?

We think of light as what we see with our eyes. Look around and you can see a wealth of colors: reds and blues, greens and yellows, browns and violets. The colors shade into one another, purple into blue into green and into yellow and orange and red. Color is not just a set of eight crayons but a continuous shading from one color into the next.

We may think of color first, but we see more than color. We see brightness as well. White is a mixture of all colors; black is a void, with no light or color. In between are all the shades of gray. Our eyes see brightness and color all at once, except when it is too dark for them to see color. The brain puts all these things together so that we can distinguish the shiny metallic red of a polished fire engine from the flat dark red of construction paper or the pink of a rose petal.

What we see is important, but light does more than let us see. Sunlight warms us, because light is a form of energy. Some people use sunlight to help heat their homes. Energy from the sun keeps our planet from turning into a giant ball of lifeless ice.

All light is not the same. Our eyes show us different colors. Those colors tell us what type of light we see. Compare a color picture with one of the same scene in black and white, and you can see how much color tells about the world. Color and brightness don't tell us everything we need to know about light, however, and they don't tell us anything about close relatives of light that our eyes can't see.

Scientists have learned that how light behaves depends on how you view it. Sometimes it seems to be waves, spreading out like ripples on a pond. Sometimes it seems to be little particles. That is why scientists talk

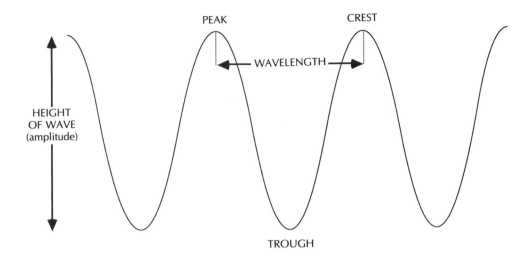

Frequency is number of waves per second

FIGURE 1-1 *A light wave has a wavelength (the distance between successive peaks) and a frequency (the number of waves passing a point per second).*

both about light waves and about light particles called "photons." For now, we'll talk about light waves, but remember that light has a dual personality; sometimes it's a wave and sometimes it's a particle. What you see depends on how you look.

Look at the light wave in Figure 1-1 and you can see it has two characteristics: its height and its wavelength, the distance between two peaks of the wave. What our eyes see as the brightness is the height of a light wave. What we see as color is the length of the wave. Neither is a perfectly accurate measurement, but they are good enough for nature.

We think of light as what we can see with our eyes. Yet visible light waves are only a small part of the whole family or spectrum of electromagnetic waves, or electromagnetic radiation. Our eyes see only a tiny part of the spectrum, as if we were looking through a thin slit between boards in a fence as in Figure 1-2. Visible light waves are very small: 2,000 would make one millimeter, and it would take 50,000 to make an inch. Some electromagnetic waves that we cannot see are much longer. Radio waves can be inches, feet, or even miles (centimeters, meters, or even kilometers) long. On the other end of the spectrum are

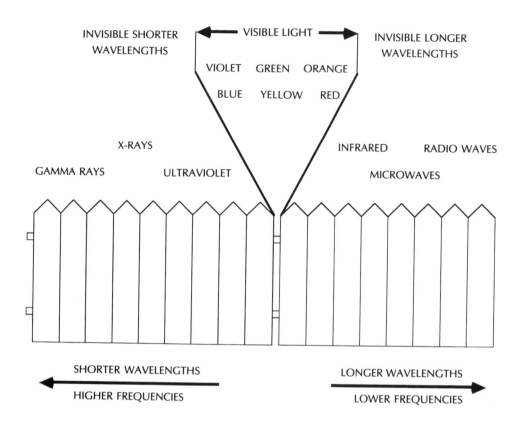

FIGURE 1–2 *Our eyes see only a small part of the whole electromagnetic spectrum, as if we were looking through a thin slit between boards in a fence.*

gamma rays, with wavelengths a million times shorter than visible light. The electromagnetic spectrum also includes X rays, microwaves, the infrared, and the ultraviolet.

To scientists, all electromagnetic waves have the same nature, just as all people are human. All waves travel at the same speed, 300,000 kilometers (180,000 miles) per second. Yet like people, electromagnetic waves differ. This book concerns only visible light and its closest relatives, the ultraviolet and the infrared. Ultraviolet wavelengths are too short for the eye to see and infrared wavelengths are too long; but otherwise they act so much like visible light that they usually are called "light," too.

Light Affects Us

Light is important because it affects us and things about us, not just because we see it. Long before animals walked the earth or developed eyes, sunlight gave energy to the first green plants. We get our energy from food that needs sunlight to grow. Sunlight warms the world during the day. The longer the sun is in the sky, the more energy the earth collects, and the warmer the weather. Differences in how much sunlight reaches the ground make the seasons change and make the earth's poles cold and the equator warm.

We use light energy in many ways. Light changes photographic film so we can see pictures. Use a lens to focus the sun's energy onto a tiny spot, and you can burn a piece of paper. Infrared light from a quartz heater can keep you warm. High-power laser light, concentrated onto small areas, can drill holes. Pulses of light passing through thin glass fibers can carry telephone calls over long distances.

People make optical tools to use light better. Some optical tools make "artificial" light to let us see where sunlight does not reach. Prehistoric people had torches and campfires. A century ago most people still used firelight from candles, lanterns, fireplaces, and gas lights. Today we have light bulbs and fluorescent lights, flashbulbs and lasers, television screens and LEDs (light-emitting diodes). Tomorrow there may be even more light sources.

Some optical tools change light. Left alone, light travels in a straight line. That's fine if you only want to brighten a room with a light bulb, but it won't let you take a photograph, see a spectrum, magnify an object, or drill a tiny hole with a laser beam. To do those jobs, you need tools that can change light's direction, such as lenses, prisms, mirrors, telescopes, binoculars, and cameras. Sometimes these tools are called simply "optics."

Optics are not magical. They rely on what happens when light meets matter. Surfaces that reflect light make mirrors. Clear materials like glass bend or "refract" light that passes from one material into another. Lenses, prisms, cameras, and binoculars depend on refraction. Your eyes also bend light, but not always perfectly, and many people need eyeglasses to help them see clearly.

You couldn't see if your eyes didn't sense or detect light. Scientists have developed other kinds of light "detectors"—photographic film, for example. Other light detectors produce electricity when light strikes them. That is how a television camera works; it converts light into an electrical signal that your television set turns back into a picture on the screen.

Optical engineers can use these optical tools to make powerful instruments. Today's telescopes can see objects so far away that their light takes billions of years to reach us. They use giant mirrors wider than you are tall and electronic detectors that can collect feeble starlight much too faint for the eye to see.

Optical tools do much more than help us see. Later in this book we'll learn how light can help cure disease, cut plastics, or send telephone calls around the world. But first we need to learn more about what light is and does.

What Light Is and Does

The Nature of Light

We have seen that light is part of the family of electromagnetic radiation or electromagnetic waves. The word *electromagnetic* indicates that the waves are partly electrical and partly magnetic. The word *radiation* is used because the waves spread, or "radiate," in all directions like ripples in a pool of water, or like the rays in Figure 2–1. (It does not mean that they are dangerous, radioactive, or have anything to do with nuclear power or weapons.)

All electromagnetic waves share some traits. All behave like waves at some times and like particles at others. All travel at the same speed in empty space, 300,000 kilometers (180,000 miles) per second. They go almost as fast in air. That means light can reach us from anywhere on the earth faster than we can sense. Light takes only about a second to go from the earth to the moon. It is much faster than sound (which is why you see a distant flash of lightning before you hear the thunder that goes with it). Scientists believe the speed of light is a universal speed limit, and that nothing can go faster.

Every electromagnetic wave has a wavelength, the distance from one peak to the next, as shown in Figure 1–1. If you know the wave-

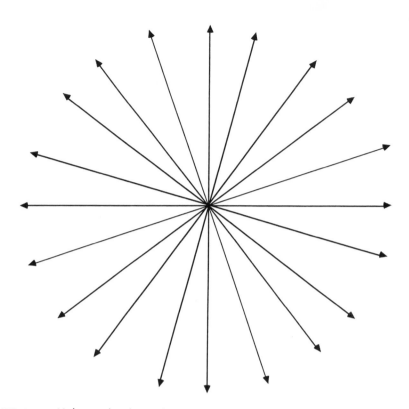

FIGURE 2–1 *Light and other electromagnetic waves radiate in all directions from a point.*

length, you can tell how the wave will act. Scientists use wavelengths to identify the members of the family of electromagnetic waves, which are listed in Table 2–1. Wavelengths are always measured in metric units.

There is a wide range of wavelengths, so Table 2–1 lists some measurement terms that you wil not recognize. Visible light has wavelengths of 0.000,0004 to 0.000,0007 meter, too small to see, and much smaller than anything you have ever measured. Because nobody wants to write all those zeros, scientists measure light wavelength in nanometers, where *nano* means billionth. That makes the wavelengths of visible light 400 to 700 nanometers, numbers that look much nicer.

You probably have already met some metric prefixes, such as *milli* for thousandth and *kilo* for thousand. Table 2–2 lists the metric prefixes used to measure light and their meanings. Remember that nanometers (abbreviated nm) mean billionths of a meter and kilometer means thousands of meters—so 400 nanometers means 400 billionths of a meter or 0.000,000,400 meter. It may take a while to learn these prefixes, but they make the numbers much easier to write.

Wavelength is closely related to another measurement called "frequency," which is the number of wave peaks passing a point in a second. Frequency is measured in Hertz (abbreviated Hz), a unit named for Heinrich Hertz, the scientist who discovered radio waves a century ago. The frequencies of electromagnetic waves also are listed in Table 2–1. Note that the higher the frequency, the shorter the wavelength. Multiply frequency by wavelength and you always get the same answer—the speed of light.

TABLE 2–1   *Wavelengths and Frequencies of Electromagnetic Waves*

TYPE OF WAVE	WAVELENGTHS	FREQUENCIES
Gamma rays*	under 0.003 nm	over 100,000,000 THz
X rays*	0.003–10 nm	30,000–100,000,000 THz
Ultraviolet light*	10–400 nm	750–30,000 THz
Visible light	400–700 nm	420–750 THz
Infrared light	700 nm–1 mm	300–420,000 GHz
Microwaves†	1 mm–30 cm	1–300 GHz
Radio waves†	30 cm–30,000 m	10 kHz–1 GHz
Low-frequency waves‡	over 30 km	under 10 kHz

*The boundaries between the ultraviolet, X rays, and gamma rays are not well defined. Other sources may give different values.
†Sometimes microwaves are grouped with radio waves.
‡This part of the spectrum is not well defined and is little used.

So far we have talked only about light waves, but light also acts like particles. The particle side of light's personality becomes important in carrying energy. The energy comes in tiny chunks, which are called "photons."

Normally, we see so much light that the photons all come together,

TABLE 2–2   *Prefixes Used with Metric Units for Wavelength and Frequency*

PREFIX	ABBREVIATION	MEANING	NUMBER
tera	T	trillion	1,000,000,000,000
giga	G	billion	1,000,000,000
mega	M	million	1,000,000
kilo	k	thousand	1,000
deci	d	tenth	0.1
centi	c	hundredth	0.01
milli	m	thousandth	0.001
micro	μ (Greek mu)	millionth	0.000,001
nano	n	billionth	0.000,000,001
pico	p	trillionth	0.000,000,000,001

the way many raindrops make a stream or many grains of sand make a beach. You see grains of sand, or photons, only if you look very closely.

Photons are more like grains of sand than drops of water because they are basic chunks of light energy that you can't break down. Photon energy depends on frequency and wavelength. The shorter the wavelength and higher the frequency, the higher the photon energy. Look at Table 2–1, and you will find the waves with highest energy (and shortest wavelength) at the top and those with lowest energy at the bottom. Some scientists use photon energy to measure electromagnetic waves, but we will stick to wavelength because it's simpler. Mostly we will use nanometers (nm), but elsewhere you may meet micrometers (μm, millionths of a meter), microns (slang for micrometers), or Ångstroms (Å, tenths of a nanometer).

You probably have seen what many people call light rays when sunlight sneaks between clouds or comes through a window or some other opening. Later in this book, we will talk about different light rays, which are the paths that light waves take. They are straight lines that change direction only when light goes from one material into another.

Absorption, Reflection, and Transmission

We have seen what light is by itself. What happens when light meets something else? Any of three things. The object can absorb the light, reflect it, or let it pass through. Most things do some of each, as shown in Figure 2–2.

When you sit in a sunny spot and feel the warmth of the sun, you absorb light. The light energy enters your body and stays there (at least for a while). Different things absorb different amounts of light. Black paper absorbs most light that hits it, while white paper absorbs little. All matter absorbs some light, but some things—such as air, mirrors, and glass—absorb too little to be noticeable.

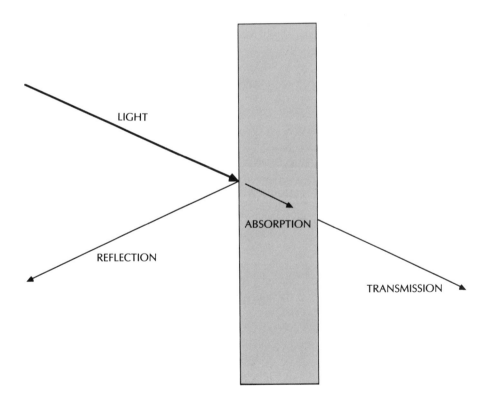

FIGURE 2–2 *Objects absorb, reflect, and transmit light.*

Some light energy never enters an object because it is reflected from the surface. You can think of the light waves as balls bouncing off a wall. Mirrors aren't the only objects that reflect light. Every surface reflects some light, but they reflect different amounts in different ways. We see most things by reflected light, so how they look depends on the colors they reflect.

Light that is neither absorbed nor reflected is transmitted—that is, it passes through the object. We think of glass and air as transmitting light, but other things do, too. Hold a thin piece of paper in front of a light, and some light will leak through.

This page is a good example of something that absorbs, reflects, and transmits light. The dark print absorbs light. The white paper reflects it. And if you hold it up to a bright light, some light can pass through. Your hand also absorbs, reflects, and transmits light. Hold it close to a light bulb, and you can feel it absorb light energy. Look at it, and you can see that it reflects light. Hold your fingers together over a lighted flashlight, and you can see some red light leak through the places where your fingers touch, because your skin transmits some light.

Something that blocks most light is called "opaque," and something you can see through clearly is called "transparent." A wall is opaque, and a window is transparent. Something that lets some light through but is not clear is called "translucent"; wax paper and tissue paper are examples.

Reflection, absorption, and transmission all depend on wavelength. Objects usually absorb, transmit, and reflect some wavelengths more than others. That is why we see colors. A green leaf looks green because it reflects more green light than other wavelengths. If something reflects more red light than other wavelengths, it looks red. Paper looks white because it reflects most light at visible wavelengths; ink looks black because it absorbs most visible light.

Likewise, colored glass or plastic gets its color because it transmits only some visible wavelengths. Red glass, for example, transmits red light but not green, as you can see if you look through a piece at colored Christmas lights. Glass, water, and air are clear because they transmit all visible wavelengths, but they are not transparent to all invisible elec-

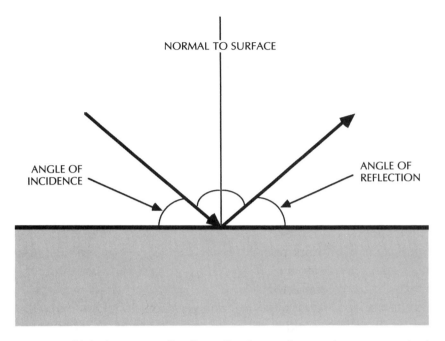

FIGURE 2–3 *Light bounces off a flat reflective surface at the same angle that it hits, so the angle of incidence equals the angle of reflection.*

tromagnetic waves. The only thing that doesn't absorb electromagnetic waves at any wavelength is nothing—empty space.

Types of Reflection

Reflection varies with more than wavelength. It also varies with the type of surface.

The simplest type of surface is perfectly flat. Reflection from such a surface is shown in Figure 2–3. The light bounces off the surface at an angle of reflection equal to the angle at which the light struck it, called the "angle of incidence." The same thing would happen if a ball bounced off a wall. Here we show the angles measured from the surface, but scientists measure the angles from a "normal" at a right angle (90 degrees) to the surface. It doesn't matter for this kind of reflection, but it does for some other optical effects.

Reflection like this from a flat surface is what makes a mirror. If you

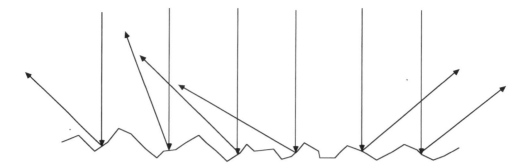

FIGURE 2–4 *Diffuse reflection is from a surface that looks rough to light waves (like white paper).*

look straight at a mirror, the light from your face bounces back at you, and you see your reflection. That does not happen with white, paper, even though it too reflects light.

White paper looks smooth to our eyes, but it isn't smooth to light. Remember that light waves are only about ½₀₀₀th of a millimeter long. To them, the surface of paper appears rough, as in Figure 2–4. This rough surface scatters light in all directions, in what is called "diffuse reflection." The shiny reflection of a mirror is called "specular reflection." We will learn more about how specular reflection makes images in the next chapter.

Transparency and Refraction

Transparent materials do more than transmit light. They also bend its path, or *refract* light. Eyeglasses, a magnifying lens, and a clear glass filled with water all refract light as it goes from one transparent material into another, such as from air into glass, or glass into water.

Refraction happens because light travels at different speeds in different materials. It goes fastest through empty space, and almost as fast through air. It travels more slowly through water, and even more slowly through glass. When light goes from air into glass, it is slowed down, but its frequency and color stay the same. That makes its wavelength shorter and bends the light as it enters the glass, as shown in Figure 2–5. The larger the difference in speeds in two materials, the more light is bent as it goes between them.

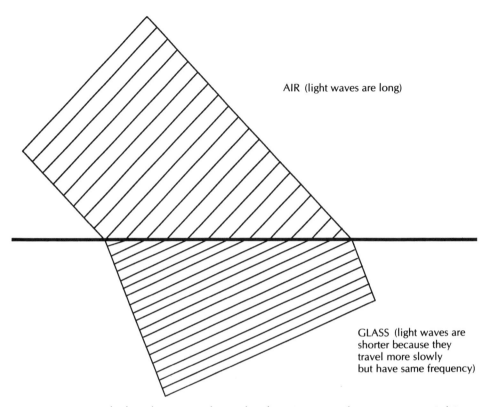

AIR (light waves are long)

GLASS (light waves are
shorter because they
travel more slowly
but have same frequency)

FIGURE 2–5 *Light bends (or is refracted) when it passes from one material into another. The speed changes, but the frequency stays the same, so the peaks (shown by the lines) are closer together in the material where light travels more slowly. The light changes direction to keep the peaks of the wave aligned in the two materials.*

To measure how much a material can bend light, we use a number called the "refractive index," which is the speed of light in empty space divided by the speed of light in the material. The refractive index of air is very close to 1, that of water is 1.3, and that of ordinary glass is about 1.5. That means that light travels through glass two-thirds as fast as through air.

How much light bends at a surface also depends on the angle at which it hits. If it strikes the surface straight-on, at the ninety-degree "normal" angle, it does not bend at all. If it goes from a low-index material (like air) into a higher-index material (like glass), it bends toward the normal. If it goes from a high-index material into a lower-index one, it bends away from the normal. In other words, Figure 2–5 works if light is going in either direction.

You can see refraction in action in many places: eyeglasses, magnifiers, or even in a clear drinking glass full of water. You don't see refraction in flat window glass because light bends in opposite directions as it goes through the two flat surfaces. Even air refracts light, which makes the sun set a little later and rise a little earlier than it would on a planet with no air. As we will see in the next chapter, refraction is used in many optical instruments.

Light Scattering

Another thing that can happen to light is scattering. One example is the diffuse reflection from white paper shown in Figure 2–4. Light waves also scatter in many directions when they pass through air full of dust or tiny water droplets. Look up on a cloudy day and you can't see the sun; drops in the clouds have scattered its light all over the sky. Even on a clear day, tiny dust particles in the air scatter shorter wavelengths, and that scattered light colors the sky blue. Light from the setting sun must go through so much air that most of the blue and green can't reach your eyes. The longer-wavelength red light does get through, so the setting sun looks red.

Interference

Light waves can sometimes do strange things, like canceling each other out, as shown in Figure 2–6. This is one reason scientists thought light was a wave. If two waves have the same wavelength, and their peaks line up with each other, they add together to make a stronger wave and a brighter light. However, if the peaks of one wave line up with the valleys of the other, one wave subtracts from the other, making the light fainter. If the waves are the same height, this "interference" can cancel the waves, making a dark spot where they come together.

Interference effects are uncommon but striking when you see them. As we'll see in the next chapter, they can even make a rainbow pattern of colors when light strikes a pattern of many fine, parallel lines.

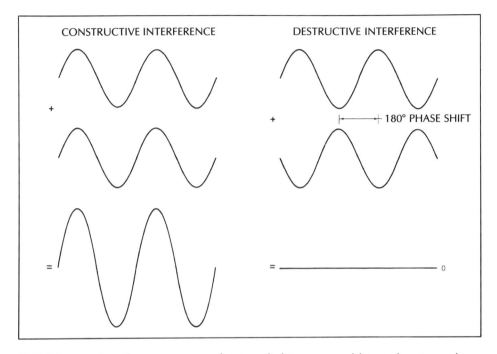

FIGURE 2–6 *Interference can make two light waves add together to make a bright spot or cancel each other out to make a dark spot, depending on how the peaks and valleys of the waves line up. (Reproduced with permission of the publisher, Howard W. Sams & Co., Indianapolis, Indiana, from* Understanding Fiber Optics, *Jeff Hecht, copyright © 1987)*

Simple Optics and How They Work

Light was magical to prehistoric peoples. Many of them worshipped the sun because they knew it was the source of light and heat. Knowing how to control light—even just how to reflect it—gave them power. A shiny rock that we would think a very poor mirror was magical to them. One of the first allures of gold must have been its brightness in the sun. As ancient peoples discovered new metals, they used them not just for tools but also for mirrors, and they buried some of those mirrors with their kings and queens.

Today we know that light is really not magic, but we can still be fascinated by what simple optics can do to light. Think of how people sometimes say something hard is "done with mirrors." Watch a baby play with a mirror, or go into a carnival hall of mirrors and see the strange versions of you the mirrors reflect. In this chapter we will see how mirrors, lenses, and other simple optics use the laws of reflection and refraction to control light.

Focusing Light

Nature has given us a few rocks that are shiny or clear, but metals and glass were the key to mirrors and lenses. They go back thousands of years, though no one was kind enough to record their discovery. They probably were made by accident, when the right rocks were heated in a fire. Glass probably was first found in sand where a fire had burned. The oldest glass dates from about 2000 B.C., but clear glass was not made until hundreds of years later.

Ancient metalsmiths and glassmakers kept their art a secret, and history says little about them. Somewhere in ancient times, people found that a curved mirror or rounded piece of glass could bring the sun's rays together, focusing them onto a small spot. They found, too, that this intense light could set leaves or other dry tinder on fire. On a sunny day, you can use a magnifier a few centimeters (an inch or two) across to perform this ancient bit of magic by focusing sunlight onto paper. (Dark paper works best, and be careful because you can set the paper on fire quickly.)

The Greeks and Catoptrics

The ancient Greeks were the first to try to make optics a science. They wrote of light rays, which they knew went straight except when bent or reflected at surfaces. Being skillful mathematicians, they treated *catoptrics* as a kind of geometry. They devised a simple experiment you can do to show refraction. Put a coin into an empty cup, and put the cup on a table or counter just far enough away so you can't see the coin. If someone fills the cup with water, the water will bend the light rays enough for you to see the coin again, as shown in Figure 3–1.

The Greeks knew how to make mirrors do things wondrous to them, such as seeing their own backs, seeing themselves upside down, or distorting their features. They probably knew how to use glass or crystal to focus the sun's light. Yet they did few practical things with light, had incorrect ideas about refraction, and were totally wrong about how vision works.

One intriguing optical legend has reached us from ancient times. It

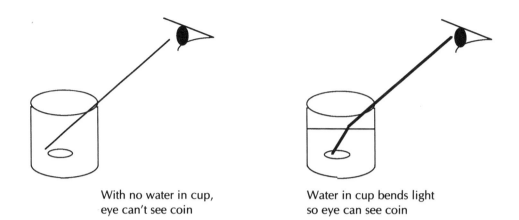

With no water in cup,
eye can't see coin

Water in cup bends light
so eye can see coin

FIGURE 3–1 *If there is no water in the cup, the eye can't see the coin. Water in the cup bends light so rays from the coin can reach the eye. The ancient Greeks used this simple experiment to show refraction.*

tells how Archimedes, one of the greatest ancient Greek mathematicians and scientists, may have used light as a weapon in a war his city of Syracuse fought with Rome. The city was under siege in 212 B.C., its harbor full of Roman ships out of range of Syracuse's soldiers.

The legend says that Archimedes made a set of mirrors, which focused sunlight onto the Roman ships and set them on fire. If that cost the Romans a battle, it did not cost them the war. Roman soldiers conquered the city, and—despite an order from their general—killed Archimedes.

Many scholars doubt the story, and some have said flatly it would have been impossible. Yet over 200 years ago, French scientist George Louis Leclerc de Buffon ignited wooden planks 150 feet (46 meters) away with an array of 168 mirrors, each 6 by 8 inches (15 by 20 centimeters). That did not prove that Archimedes did burn the Roman ships—mirrors were hard to make in his day—but it did show the deed was not impossible.

Mirrors as Optics

Whatever Archimedes did, it is clear that the Greeks understood how mirrors worked. Legend says that Archimedes used many small flat mirrors, and those are the simplest type. If you're standing in front of a flat mirror, the mirror sends light right back at you. That makes objects you see in the mirror look as far behind the mirror as they are away from it, so if your face is a foot from the mirror, it looks as if it's a foot behind the mirror (or two feet away from you). The reflection reverses right and left, making what we call a mirror image. To see how a mirror image is reversed, write a letter F on tracing paper and hold it between yourself and the mirror. The F in the mirror looks the same as the F you see through the paper, as shown in Figure 3–2. However, the F on the side of the paper *facing* the mirror faces the other way.

To focus light to a point a mirror must be curved, as shown in Figure 3–3. When parallel light rays (from something far away, like the sun)

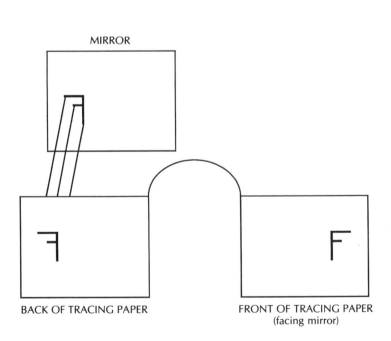

FRONT OF TRACING PAPER
(facing mirror)

BACK OF TRACING PAPER

FIGURE 3–2 *How right and left are reversed in a mirror image: it depends on your point of view.*

FIGURE 3–3 *A concave mirror focuses parallel rays to its focal point. Light rays coming from a nearby object are not parallel and are focused to form a real image.*

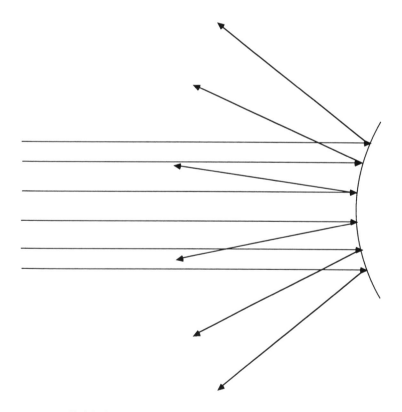

FIGURE 3–4 *Parallel light rays spread out after reflection from a convex mirror.*

bounce off such a *concave* mirror, they are focused to a point, called the "focal point." The distance between the mirror and this point is called the "focal length." If the light rays are not perfectly parallel but come from a nearby object, after they bounce off the mirror they will come together to form an "image" of the object. The image will be farther away from the mirror than the focal length.

What if the mirror is curved the other way, outward instead of inward? This is called a "convex" mirror, and it reflects light in a different way. Parallel light rays that strike this mirror's surface diverge, or spread out from each other, as shown in Figure 3–4.

Although convex mirrors do not bring light rays together, they still have a focal length. All light rays reflected from a convex mirror seem to come from the same point behind it. The focal length is the distance from the mirror to that point. To show that the focal point is behind the mirror, the focal length is given as a negative number, such as − 10 centimeters.

To see how concave and convex mirrors work, look at a shiny spoon. The hollow bowl is concave; the rounded bottom convex. A spoon isn't a very good mirror, but a shallow one will give you an idea how concave and convex mirrors work. (Most concave and convex mirrors have spherical shapes like slices of a hollow ball.)

You see different things in concave and convex mirrors. Close up, a concave mirror makes your eye look larger than life. Move it farther from you, and the image blurs, then reappears, upside down and looking smaller, after you are more than the mirror's focal length away from it. On the other hand, a convex mirror always makes things look smaller than real life, no matter how far you are from it, and the image does not blur as you move away from it. We'll explain more about the types of images you see shortly.

The spoon is not flat or spherical, so it bends your image in strange ways, or *distorts* it. Trick mirrors also are bent, so they distort your image—to make you look taller or shorter, or thinner or fatter.

Real and Virtual Images

We have seen how mirrors can make images. So can other optical devices. Before we move on to those other optics, we need to learn about images. There are two kinds, called "real" and "virtual" images. Real images are things that you can project on a screen, like a movie. Virtual images are images that your eye seems to see but that can't be shown on a screen. The difference is important.

Movie projectors, cameras, telescopes, overhead projectors, and slide projectors all form real images. So do concave mirrors and magnifying lenses. The simplest way for you to make a real image is with a magnifying lens. Hold the lens directly above a light bulb that is turned on (being careful not to burn your finger on the hot bulb). Look up at the ceiling, and move the lens up and down. When the distance between the lens and the bulb is right, the lens will project an image of the bulb onto the ceiling, and you should see the bulb's label clearly.

Experimenting with the lens and the light bulb, or watching someone fumble with a projector, shows something else. A real image must be focused precisely or it will fade into a blur. This is because a real image forms only at a certain distance from a concave mirror or magnifying lens, where the light rays form a miniature (or enlarged) version of the object. Move too far in either direction and the light rays spread apart, blurring the image. That's what happens when a projector is out of focus.

A virtual image is something you can see. However, it cannot be projected on a screen because the light rays really do not come together to form a miniature version of the object. Reflection or refraction fools your eye into thinking the image is there, even though it isn't. Look in a flat mirror, and you will see a virtual image of your face. You know your face is not really behind the mirror, and the light rays can't get there, because the mirror reflects them. But the reflection fools your eyes.

By the way, your eyes can't see a real image; they just see a blur. Remember when you saw the blur in the concave-spoon mirror? That blur was the real image. You can see a real image—in a sense—if the image is projected onto a screen that reflects the light to your eye. But you couldn't see a real image projected *onto* your eyes.

Anything that reflects or refracts light can form a virtual image, but only a few optical devices can make real images. The most important are the concave mirror and the positive lens (described below), which are used in projectors, telescopes, cameras, microscopes, and much other optical equipment.

Refraction and Lenses

We saw in the last chapter that light is refracted at the surface of a transparent material, such as water, glass, or clear plastic. The shape of the surface controls the bending of light. The surface of a lens is made smooth to bend light evenly, but the surface of a drinking glass or bottle is not, so they bend light unevenly. This makes the bottom of a glass fun to look through but not very useful. If you needed eyeglasses, you wouldn't want lenses that made the world look strange.

The curved sides of practical lenses are *spherical,* shaped like parts of a hollow ball. The surfaces of high-quality optics must be so smooth that any bumps must be smaller than the wavelength of light. That means the surface must be accurate to within about one ten-thousandth of a millimeter. It isn't easy, but optics makers can routinely make lenses that accurate.

Optics specialists divide lenses into two categories: positive lenses, which can make objects look larger, and negative lenses, which always make objects look smaller. Let's look at each of these in turn.

POSITIVE LENSES

The center of a positive lens is thicker than its outer edges. As shown in Figure 3–5, this makes it bend light toward its center. If many parallel light rays pass through a positive lens, they will be focused at the focal point. The distance between the lens and the focal point is the focal length.

Light rays are parallel only if they come from a distant object. Suppose we look at something close to us. Look back at Figure 3–5 to see what happens. Light from the whole arrow goes through the lens, but to make the drawing clear, we show only a few rays. The rays passing through different parts of the lens are bent differently, but eventually come together to form an image of the arrow. This is the real image we

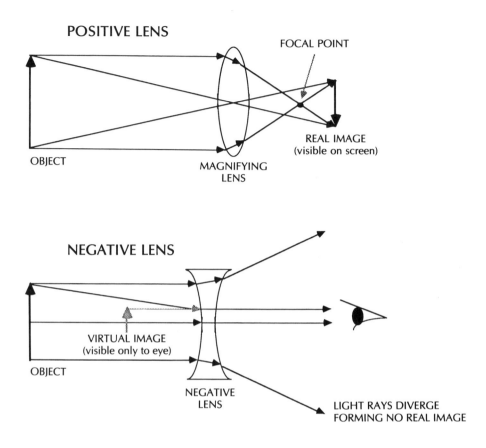

FIGURE 3–5 *A real image exists at one point where light rays come together to form an image of the object that you can see on a screen or wall. Light rays from the top and bottom of the object are brought to the corresponding places on the image. Light rays do not have to be brought together for your eyes to see a virtual image. A positive or magnifying lens makes a real image; a negative or shrinking lens makes only a virtual image.*

learned about earlier. Note that it is farther from the lens than the focal point.

Our example shows the real image smaller than the arrow, but it also can be larger than the object. You can see that by pretending that the small arrow is the object and light is going in the other direction to form an image larger than life. This is what happens with a movie projector, or when you project the label from a light bulb onto the ceiling. If the image is closer to the lens than the object, it will be smaller than life; if it is farther away than the object, it will be larger. You could see this with the image of the light-bulb label if you held your lens close enough to the ceiling, but it's much easier to see by holding the lens close to the wall in the evening while a lamp is on. You should see a tiny image of the lamp projected on the wall.

A positive lens can magnify objects closer than the focal length, which is why it's often called a magnifier. Figure 3–6 shows how this works. Light rays coming from the arrow are bent so they spread out less rapidly, as shown at the top. The eye still sees the object as being the same distance, but the way the light is spreading makes it seem to come from a larger object, as shown at the bottom. This magnification does not make a real image, just a virtual image that cannot be projected. It only works for an object closer to the lens than its focal length. If the object is farther from the lens than the focal length, it seems to be upside down, with its apparent size depending on distance between it and the lens.

All positive lenses are thicker in the middle than on the edges and have at least one side that is convex, or curved outward. However, not all positive lenses are convex on both sides. Some are flat on one side and called "plano-convex." Others are curved in (*concave*) on one side

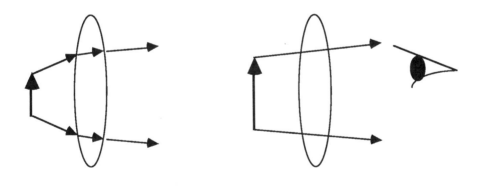

Positive lens bends light rays
from small object
so they spread out less rapidly

The eye does not realize
that the light rays have been bent,
so it sees the object as magnified

FIGURE 3–6 *A positive lens makes an object look larger.*

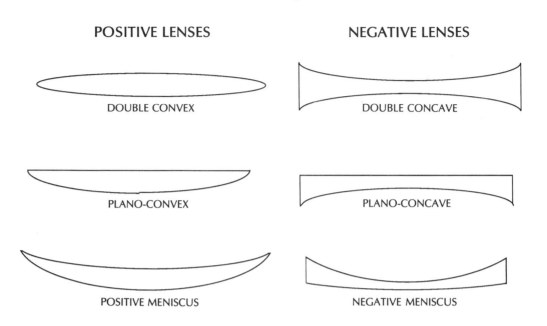

FIGURE 3–7 *Types of positive and negative lenses.*

and curved out on the other, a type called the "meniscus." These are shown in Figure 3–7.

NEGATIVE LENSES

A negative lens is the optical opposite of a positive lens. Like a convex mirror it bends parallel light rays outward, as we saw in Figure 3–5. Its center is thinner than the outside edges, and it makes objects seen through it look smaller. Like a convex mirror, its focal point is the point from which the light rays seem to come behind the lens. Because the focal point is behind the lens, the focal length is given a minus sign, and such lenses are called negative.

A negative lens makes objects seem smaller because it makes light spread outward more rapidly, fooling the eye into thinking it sees a smaller object. This happens no matter how far your eyes and the object are from the lens (although the amount of shrinking does depend on the distances). Negative lenses do not form real images because they do not bend light rays together.

There are three types of negative lenses shown in Figure 3–7, which are similar to the three types of positive lenses. Double-concave lenses have both sides curved inward. Plano-concave lenses have one side curved inward. Negative meniscus lenses have one side curved outward slightly and the other curved inward more sharply.

PINHOLE LENSES AND PINHEAD MIRRORS

There is one type of lens that doesn't contain any glass at all. It's a pinhole lens, which focuses light through a very tiny hole. It works, as shown in Figure 3–8, because all light rays from the object must go through the same tiny hole. This lets them form a real image, but a very faint one because very little light gets through the hole. A pinhole lens has very few practical uses, but it can be used to project an image of the sun by poking a hole in a box. The image will appear on the wall of the box opposite the pinhole. (If you do this experiment, look only at the image on the box. *Never* look directly at the sun because it can damage your vision.)

A mirror tiny enough will work like a pinhole lens and form a real image because the light rays are all reflected from the same small spot. Some people call such mirrors "pinhead mirrors."

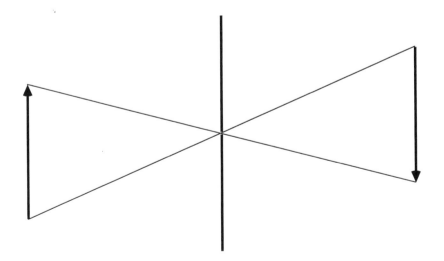

FIGURE 3–8 *Light rays passing through a tiny pinhole form a faint real image.*

Prisms, the Rainbow, and the Spectrum

In the last chapter we mentioned that how light behaves depends on its wavelength. Differences in reflection give objects their color. Differences in refraction let us see the spectrum and the rainbow.

The simplest way to see how a spectrum is made is to look at a slab of glass called a prism, as shown in Figure 3–9. Suppose all colors reach the prism at the same angle, as white light. The refractive index of glass is higher for blue light than for red. That means that the prism bends blue light more than red, so when the light emerges from the prism, it is spread out into the spectrum. Each wavelength leaves the prism at a slightly different angle.

If you have a prism, you can use it to spread out a sunbeam or light from a bright bulb into a rainbow on the wall. Look carefully at the light coming from the prism, and you will see that, as in Figure 3–9, the prism has bent the light so the spectrum isn't in a straight line with the sunbeam. Turn the prism, and the spectrum moves on the wall, but not always at the same speed with which you turn the prism. If you were to look through the prism at a light (but *never* at the sun) from where the

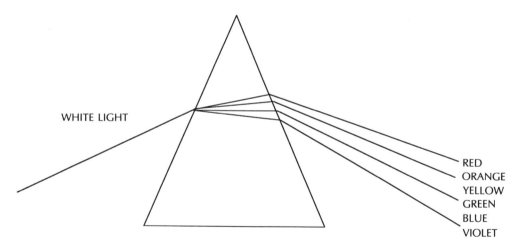

FIGURE 3–9 *A prism breaks up white light into colors because how much it bends light depends on wavelength. The shorter the wavelength, the more the light is bent.*

spectrum comes out, you would see only one color. That is because the spectrum is really spread out on your face, and only one color is on your eyes. Move your eye or turn the prism and the color will change.

Nature doesn't use glass prisms to make the rainbow. It uses many tiny droplets of water, which act like prisms to spread out the spectrum of colors. You can make your own rainbow by spraying a fine mist of water from a hose at the proper angle to the sun.

Diffraction Gratings and the Spectrum

The interference effects we mentioned in the last chapter also can produce a spectrum in a very different way from a prism. When white light is scattered from many close parallel grooves, the light waves interfere with each other so that at certain angles, all but one wavelength cancels out. The parallel grooves are called a "diffraction grating," and they produce a spectrum that looks just like one from a prism. The details are too complicated to worry about here, but diffraction gratings are important because they are easier to make and cheaper than prisms. If you can find an inexpensive one in a slide mount, it will let you see which colors are in the light given by colored bulbs, street lamps, or fluorescent lights.

A shiny surface covered with many parallel grooves makes a good diffraction grating, but the grooves do not have to be perfectly parallel or even complete. If you have ever looked at a compact disk (CD) record, or at a videodisk, you probably have seen a spectrum produced by diffraction. Those disks contain many rows of dots, aligned closely enough to act like a diffraction grating. The dots are a code that a laser beam reads to play music or video programs.

Aberrations and Complex Lenses

So far, we've pretended that simple lenses can focus light perfectly. Optical engineers know better. From the side, simple lenses look somewhat triangular, like prisms, and like a prism the angle at which they bend light depends on the wavelength. You can see this if you look through the side of a sharply curved lens at a small white object or distant white light. One side will be reddish and the other side will be blue because the two colors are refracted differently.

Simple lenses are good enough for many jobs, but not for all. Optical engineers can make more complex lenses for more demanding jobs. They combine two or more lenses, gluing them together or mounting them in a single housing. For example, the problem of a lens focusing different colors at different points can be solved by gluing together two lenses made of glass with different refractive indexes. Such a compound lens is called "achromatic," because it avoids *chromatic,* or color, distortion.

Lenses also can suffer from other optical defects, or *aberrations.* Such aberrations are too complex to describe here, but you should know that they exist and that they can affect the workings of some of the optical instruments we describe later. First, however, we will look at a natural optical instrument—the eye.

The Eye and How It Works

To most of us, light means seeing, and seeing is the king of our senses. Seeing and vision are so important to us that we use the words in many ways that have nothing to do with light. We say we *see* when we mean we understand. We have *visions* in our thoughts. To be *blind* to something is to be unaware of it.

Because light is all around us, we and other animals use it to guide us about the world. Nature gave us our own personal optical instruments, our eyes. Nerves wire them directly to the brain, and together our eyes and brain shape our view of the world. We may think of vision as simple because it is natural to us. It isn't. Scientists do not yet know all the details of how vision works. Nor can engineers build machines that can see as well as people. Computers can do arithmetic faster than people, but they cannot recognize faces as fast. To learn how vision works, we will start with the eye and see how it reacts to light, then learn how it tells the brain about the light and how the brain uses that information to make us see.

Your eye is a complex organ. You see only its outer part, shown in Figure 4–1, in a mirror. Its job is to let light in and keep other things out.

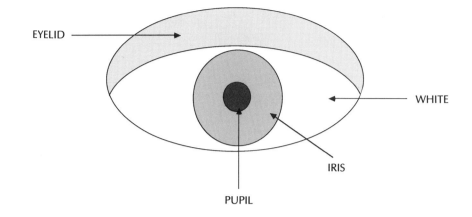

FIGURE 4–1 *The outside of the eye, what you see in the mirror.*

The eye itself is a round ball inside your skull. The inside, which you can't see in a mirror, does the seeing.

The eyelid is a protective cover with many jobs. It shuts out light when you sleep, although some light leaks through, as you can see if you close your eyes and look at a bright light. It shuts automatically if something comes toward your eye. And it keeps the surface of the eye wet by blinking regularly.

The white of the eye is the flexible outside of the eyeball and doesn't play any role in seeing. The central black circle is the pupil, which lets light enter the eye. The colored ring is the iris, which opens and closes to control how much light enters the eye. Turn a light off and on as you look in a mirror, and you can see that when it gets dark, the iris opens to let more light into the eye so you can see better.

You can learn more about how the eye sees by looking inside, as shown in Figure 4–2. Before light can enter the pupil, it must go through the eye's clear outer skin, the cornea, which also covers the iris. The cornea is what your eyelid and tear ducts keep wet. Under the cornea is the aqueous humor, a thin, watery liquid. Light then passes through the lens of the eye, which focuses it onto the back of the eyeball. The eyeball is filled with a thick, clear liquid, the vitreous humor. We sense light only when it reaches the retina, a thin layer of cells on the back of the eyeball. When light strikes the retina, it sends signals down a network of nerves to the brain, which interprets them to form the images we see.

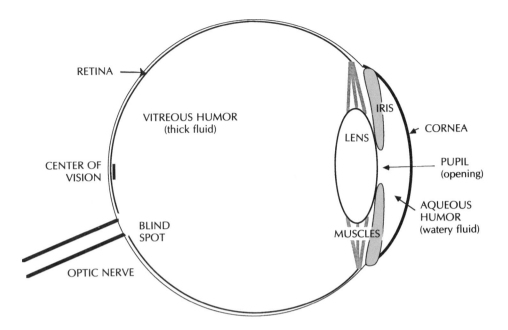

RETINA

VITREOUS HUMOR
(thick fluid)

IRIS

LENS

CORNEA

CENTER OF
VISION

PUPIL
(opening)

BLIND
SPOT

AQUEOUS
HUMOR
(watery fluid)

MUSCLES

OPTIC NERVE

FIGURE 4–2 *A view inside the eye, showing what the left eye would look like if cut open side to side.*

That is a simple picture of how the eye works, but it does not explain such details as why people need eyeglasses, how we see in color, or how we can tell distances. To learn about those important parts of vision, we need to look closer.

Focusing

When the eye focuses light properly onto the retina, it bends light rays so they form a tiny real image at the back of the eye, as shown in Figure 4–3. (You can see this real image because it is formed inside the eye.) All parts of the eye bend light some, but the cornea and the lens do the most bending. The lens automatically changes shape to focus light sharply onto the retina so you can see objects clearly.

Why are those changes necessary? Because without changing, the eye could not focus light from objects at different distances. Suppose you try to focus a real image with a simple positive lens. The closer the object is to the lens, the farther away is the image. You can't expand your eye if you bring an object closer to you, but you can change the shape of your

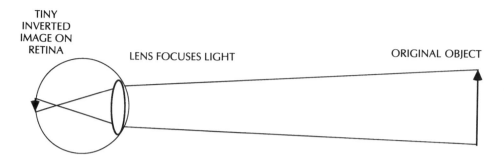

FIGURE 4–3 *The eye forms a real image of a distant object on the back of the eyeball, which the retina senses.*

lens, so it bends light more strongly. Your eye tries to do this automatically, but it can't work if things come too close. You can see that by holding your arm straight out, then bringing your finger closer to your eye until it blurs.

Your eyes cannot adjust to see everything clearly. They can't adjust to focus objects at different distances at the same time. Look out a window at distant trees, and you can see either the edge of the window or the trees clearly, but not both at the same time.

Many people's eyes cannot focus light as well as they should. Farsighted people cannot see objects close to them, whereas nearsighted people cannot see distant objects. Eyeglasses or contact lenses can correct these vision defects by bending light before it enters the eye so it will focus sharply on the retina, as shown in Figure 4–4 for a nearsighted eye. We take eyeglasses for granted today, but they were a marvelous invention to people seven hundred years ago. Today many people take off their glasses for photographs, but long ago important people often posed for paintings wearing eyeglasses.

Your eyes, like the rest of your body, change as you grow older. Not many children younger than six or seven need glasses, but as people get older, the shape of their eyes changes and defects in vision may become more serious. (The changes are slow and normally show up only on an eye test.) Vision stabilizes when people mature, but after the age of forty the lenses of the eyes start to get stiff, and it becomes hard to focus on objects at different distances.

The lens has to bend the most to focus on close objects, so reading without glasses becomes harder as people age. Some older people hold books farther away from them, but others may use special reading glasses that help them focus on books. Some reading glasses look like half-glasses because the people who wear them do not need help focusing on distant objects. People who normally wear glasses find that a single pair will not let them focus on both close and distant objects. One person who got frustrated with this problem was Benjamin Franklin. His solution was to cut two different lenses in half and fit half of each in front of each eye. The half-lens at the bottom adjusted his vision for close reading. The half at the top helped him see faraway objects. Such glasses are called "bifocals," and today many people wear them.

The Retina

We see an image focused onto the back of the eyeball because the retina responds to the light and transmits the impression to the brain. The retina is made of two kinds of specialized nerve cells—cones, which respond

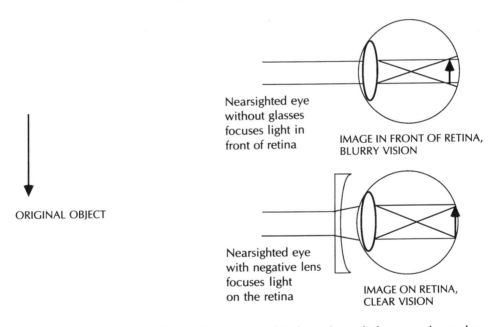

ORIGINAL OBJECT

Nearsighted eye without glasses focuses light in front of retina

IMAGE IN FRONT OF RETINA, BLURRY VISION

Nearsighted eye with negative lens focuses light on the retina

IMAGE ON RETINA, CLEAR VISION

FIGURE 4–4 *A negative lens helps a nearsighted eye focus light properly on the retina. Without glasses, the eyes focuses light in front of the retina, and vision is blurred.*

to bright light, and rods, which only work in dim light. (The names come from their shapes.)

We do most of our seeing with the eye's seven million cones. Some of them are packed closely together in the center of the retina (the fovea), where light is focused when you read or look straight ahead. The densely packed cones help you see fine details, such as the words on this page. The cones also are the part of the eye that senses colors.

The eye also contains about 125 million rods, mostly off to the sides. They can sense much fainter light than cones and let you see at night, but they do not sense colors, only black and white. Rods turn themselves off in bright light, and they take time to turn back on. This is why it takes your eyes a few minutes to get used to the dark, or *dark adapt,* if the lights go out suddenly. Once your eyes have dark adapted, a bright flash of light can leave you *night blind* until they can get used to the dark again. You might experience that if you are outside on a dark night and look at bright car headlights. Your eyes dark adapt enough to see in a minute or two, but scientists have found it takes thirty minutes to dark adapt fully.

Night vision is a little different from day vision, and because we spend most of our time in the light, night vision can have some surprises. Red objects often look much darker in dim light than blue ones, because rods are more sensitive to blue light and less sensitive to red than cones. Another surprise is that faint objects are very hard to see if you look straight at them, because the center of the retina contains very few rods. For example, look at the whole night sky, and you can see many faint stars. But many of them will vanish if you try to look straight at them! They don't really go away, but the center of your eye can't see their faint light. You can make those faint stars reappear if you learn to aim your eyes a little distance from them. This is called "averting" your vision.

Sometimes your eyes can get too much light. That's what happens when a flashbulb dazzles your eyes and you still seem to see the light for several seconds after the flash has stopped. The eye responds to light by producing chemicals, and if the light is very bright, the eye produces so much of the chemicals that it takes a long time for them to go away. A bright flash does not harm your eyes because it is very short. Neither will a momentary glance at the sun. However, staring at the sun *is* dangerous, because it can focus enough solar energy to damage the sensitive cones in the center of your retina. You would still be able to see, but you would no longer have the fine vision needed to read.

Color

Color is both beautiful and useful. Without color, the world would look dull and gray—and it would be hard to tell things apart. Take away color, and it would be hard to tell a ripe fruit from an unripe one or a red flower petal from a green leaf.

We see color because our eyes have three types of cones, which respond to different wavelengths of light. One type of cone is most sensitive to the short-wavelength blue end of the spectrum, although it does respond some to other colors. A second cone, called the green cone, is most sensitive to green light. The third is most sensitive to yellow or orange, but we call it the red cone because it is more sensitive to red light than the other cones.

Figure 4–5 shows the response of the three types of cones, along with how we define colors. The brain compares what the three cones tell it and decide what color something is. We see more than three colors because of the way the brain combines the signals it receives. If the eye gets a lot of red light and a little green light, the brain sees red-orange. Add more green light and you see yellow, but never a reddish green. The three cones let you see a whole range of colors that slowly shade from one into the other.

It may sound as if each color has its own wavelength, but it doesn't quite work that way. Figure 4–5 shows the color that your brain sees if you see each wavelength by itself. For example, your eye would see 590-nanometer light as orange. However, that isn't the only way your eye might see orange. It could see orange if it got some red light and some yellow light—without any light at all between 580 and 600 nanometers in the orange slot of the chart.

So far we have talked about what happens when light of different colors reaches your eye. This is called "additive" color mixing. Different things happen when you mix colored paints or inks together. Those materials get their colors by absorbing certain colors, subtracting them from

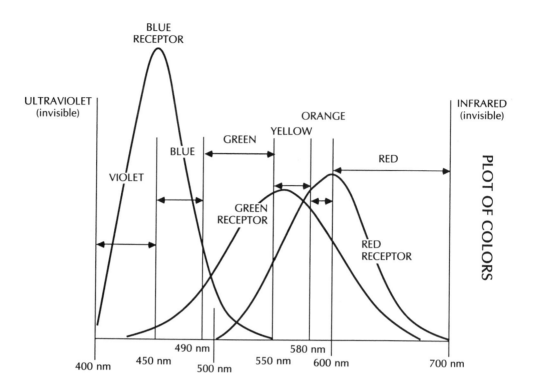

FIGURE 4–5 *The response of the eye's three types of color-sensing cones depends on the wavelength of light. The brain sees color by comparing how the cones respond. The color labels tell how each wavelength looks to your eye by itself, but they do not mean that when you see that color, you are seeing those wavelengths.*

the reflected light, so mixing paints is called "subtractive" color mixing. You can see the difference in mixing red, blue, and green. Mix lights of the three colors, and you get white, because all three colors reach the eye. Mix paints and you get a dark gray or black because the pigments together absorb most light that reaches them.

Color theory is complex, and we cannot go into much detail here. There's plenty of room to experiment if you have some pieces of colored glass or plastic and some colored lights. We saw earlier that most things get their color by reflecting light. This means that their color depends on the light that reaches them. In a room lit only by a red light, green paper will look black (because it has no green light to reflect), and red paper and white paper will look the same (because both reflect red light). Colors also will seem to change if you look through a piece of colored plastic (which gets its color because it lets through more light of one color than of others).

We take color for granted, but not everyone can see all colors. Some people are missing one receptor, making them *color-blind,* and a few people are missing two. Males are much more likely to be color-blind than females. Color-blind people missing only one receptor do see color, but not as well as people with normal vision. For example, they may not be able to tell blue from green, or red from brown, but they can tell other colors apart. Eye doctors have special charts that test for color blindness by showing patterns of colored dots. People with normal vision see a pattern, but those who are color-blind do not. Such tests are the best way to find out if one is color-blind. People who are color-blind may not realize it—which probably is a major reason why it was only about 200 years ago that scientists discovered color blindness.

The color receptors in our cones limit the colors we can see. The longest wavelengths we can see are the red and the shortest the violet. It is usually said that human vision ranges from 400 to 700 nanometers, but actually the cutoff is gradual, and it is possible to see slightly longer and shorter wavelengths because the eye responds weakly to them.

Why We See in Three Dimensions

We live in a three-dimensional world, where objects have depth as well as length and height. A photograph can show us the world, but it is missing depth. Our eyes see this three-dimensional world, even though each eye projects its image onto part of the retina that is almost flat. How does it work?

The secret is that our two eyes point in the same direction, giving us what is called "binocular vision." Although they point in the same direction, they are several centimeters (two or three inches) apart, so each eye gives a slightly different view. To see this, close one eye, stretch out your arm, raise one finger on your hand, and look at the finger and what lies beyond it. Then open that eye and close the other, and you will see that the finger seems to have moved. What has really happened is that you are looking through a different eye, which is giving you a slightly different viewpoint.

When you are conscious of the two different viewpoints, you sometimes can confuse your brain and switch between the two. Normally, however, your brain combines the two automatically in a way that helps you tell how far away objects are. This helps you get a three-dimensional view of the world. (If objects are close, your brain picks the view from one eye, so you don't see double images.)

Binocular vision is not the only clue your brain uses to tell distances. It also relies on perspective, the fact that objects seem smaller the farther away they are. Look at a flat photograph, and you know that a house that looks small is farther away than a similar house that looks large. The same happens if you look at the world with one eye, so animals without binocular vision can estimate distances. However, if you look carefully, you will see that a one-eyed view of the world is flatter than one seen with two eyes.

The Brain and Vision

Color and three-dimensional vision are two examples of how the brain and the eyes work together so we can see. The rods and cones in the retina are nerves, connected directly to the brain. The brain uses inputs from these nerves to create the images that we "see."

The brain helps us see in many other ways that we don't notice. For example, the lens forms an upside-down image on the retina, but the brain automatically turns it right-side up. Your brain also compensates for a tiny blind spot in the eye, where the optic nerve leaves the eyeball on its way to the brain, shown in Figure 4–2. There are no rods or cones there, so you never see light arriving at that spot, but since it is away from the center of your vision you normally don't notice it. To see the blind spot in action, focus your right eye on the cross in Figure 4–6 and move the page toward and away from you. When it is about six inches (fifteen centimeters) from your eye, the circle will disappear, because its image falls on your blind spot.

Our brain and eyes do other special things that we may not notice.

LOOK HERE   VANISHING SPOT

FIGURE 4–6 *Focus your right eye on the cross and move the page to and from you. When the circle falls on your blind spot, it will disappear.*

Has something moving ever caught your eye, even when you weren't looking toward it? Have you ever noticed how much easier it is to spot a moving fly than one that's resting someplace where it's easier to swat? That's because your eyes are made to spot motion. Animals also need to know when things are moving. A wild rabbit will ignore you if you sit still, but will look up and run away if you move toward it. Its eyes and brain have warned it that something is moving, and it knows that something moving could be dangerous.

Sometimes images and your eyes can play tricks on the brain, called optical illusions. If you try to estimate the lengths of the horizontal lines in Figure 4–7, you are likely to fall victim to one optical illusion. Measure them with a ruler and you'll be surprised to see which one is longer.

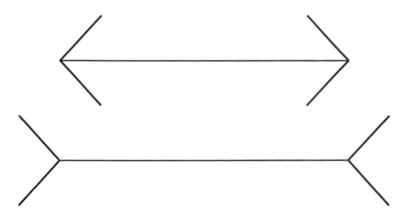

FIGURE 4–7 *Which horizontal line is longer? An optical illusion is trying to deceive your eyes. Measure the lines with a ruler, and you'll be surprised.*

Other Types of Eyes

Some animals have eyes that work much like ours, but most do not. For example, a duck's eyes are on opposite sides of its head, so the two eyes do not see the same things; the bird does not have binocular vision. Some animals have color vision, but others don't—and scientists have found no easy way to tell if an animal sees colors. A mouse can't tell you if it sees red or green; you have to experiment to see if it can tell the difference.

Blindness

Many things can go wrong with eyes. They are fragile and can be damaged if they are hit. Nature gives some protection, such as the ridge of bone around the eye, and the blink reflex that shuts the eyelid when you see something coming. But even a shut eyelid can't prevent damage from a speeding rock or pellet, so people in many jobs wear safety goggles or special glasses to keep stray objects from hurting their eyes.

Some diseases also can cause blindness. The commonest is a side effect of diabetes called "diabetic retinopathy" that makes the retina less sensitive. Treatment with a laser can slow the disease but does not always cure it, and some people who suffer from it find their vision gradually fading away. They need brighter and brighter light to see until at last they can't see at all.

As some people age, the lens of the eye grows cloudy. This is called a "cataract." Many years ago, it led to blindness, but now doctors can replace the natural lens with a clear plastic implant so cataract sufferers can see again.

Another cause of eye damage is glaucoma, a buildup of pressure in the eyeball. This can damage the retina and optic nerve, eventually causing blindness if the pressure is not relieved by drugs or an operation to let some fluid out.

Sources of Light

Most objects in our world—books, trees, people, houses, plants, animals, mountains, and so on—do not produce visible light. We see them because they reflect light from the sun or other light sources. Only a few things produce light, and that makes them something special.

We often call light sources "natural" or "artificial." Natural sources like the sun, stars, or fireflies make light without help from people. Artificial lights are things from candles to lasers made by people. However, if you look closely, you can see that natural and artificial sources often make light in similar ways, relying on the same natural laws.

Light Energy and Black Bodies

Light is a form of energy, so objects that emit light give off energy. Heat also is a form of energy. Hot things give off heat—and the hotter they are, the more heat they give off. If you suspect these facts are related, you're right, because of what we call the "black-body" law. (We'll explain the name later.)

The black-body law says that the hotter an object is, the more energy it releases as light and other electromagnetic waves. The energy released increases very rapidly with temperature. As temperature rises, the wavelengths emitted also get shorter. This makes sense because hotter objects have more energy to release, and the shorter the wavelength, the more energy an electromagnetic wave contains.

To understand what this means, watch something get very hot. At first it looks normal, even when you can start to feel heat from it. Heat it enough, and it starts to glow "red hot," like an electric heater or the heating wires in a toaster. If you heat it even more, it gets even brighter, and looks white, like the wire inside a light bulb.

What has happened? At normal temperatures everything gives off some heat energy, but not very much and not at wavelengths you can see. The peak wavelength emitted is 10,000 nanometers in the invisible infrared, twenty times longer than visible light. As the object gets hotter, it emits more energy at shorter infrared wavelengths. You can feel the infrared energy as heat, but your eyes don't see it as light. When an object gets red hot, it emits the longest visible wavelengths, red light. Heat it more, and the peak wavelength moves into the middle of the visible spectrum, and you see a mixture of colors, or white light. If you could heat the object even more, the peak wavelength would be even shorter, and it would start to look blue. At the millions of degrees of a nuclear explosion, the peak wavelength is in the very short X-ray region, but much visible light is still emitted. Table 5–1 lists a sampling of temperatures and peak wavelengths.

Why do scientists call objects that emit light "black bodies?" Because they mean "black" objects that don't reflect light, not dark objects that don't emit light. A black body may not reflect light, but it emits light energy if it is hot enough. The sun acts like such a black body.

The Sun, the Stars, and Distance

The sun is the star closest to us and like all stars shines because it is hot. The sun's surface is about 5500 degrees Celsius (roughly 10,000 degrees Fahrenheit). The brightest wavelengths in sunlight are green, in the middle of the visible spectrum. That is no accident. It makes sense that living things should use the brightest wavelengths to see.

TABLE 5–1   *Temperatures of Objects and Their Black-Body Emission*

TEMPERATURE	OBJECT	PEAK WAVELENGTH (nanometers)	COLOR TO EYE
32°C (98.6°F)	Person	10,000	—
230°C (450°F)	Hot oven	6,000	—
260–430°C (500–800°F)	Electric heating coil	5500–4100	red
2700°C (4900°F)	Light-bulb filament	1000	white*
5500°C (10,000°F)	Sun	500	white*
13,000°C (23,000°F)	Very hot star	200	blue

*Light from bulbs looks redder than sunlight

Some stars are much brighter than the sun and some much fainter, but the sun seems the brightest because it is the closest. The next-nearest star is 63,000 times farther from us than the sun—and so it seems much, much fainter. It's as if you lived in New York, the sun was a few houses away, and the next nearest star was in Los Angeles.

The stars look much more than 63,000 times fainter than the sun because light spreads out with distance. Think of light leaving a star's surface as an expanding balloon. The more it expands, the more space the same light must cover, as shown in Figure 5–1. If you double your distance from the star, the light that covered one square must cover four squares. This makes the light look much fainter farther away. In fact, the brightness of a star or other light source drops as if you were dividing by the distance times itself, so a light bulb at twice the distance looks only one-quarter as bright.

Other Natural Light Sources

There are many other natural light sources besides the sun and the stars. Planets and the moon reflect sunlight. A meteor, or "shooting star," appears when a small rock from space burns in the atmosphere, and we see

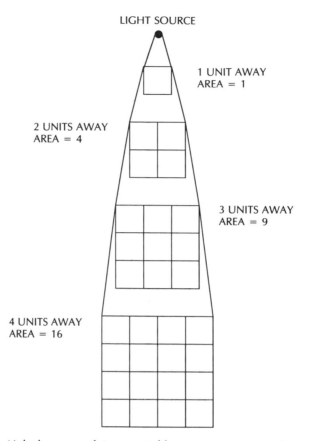

FIGURE 5–1 *Light becomes fainter quickly as it moves away from a light source. The same light that covers one square at one unit distance from a star is spread over four squares at twice the distance, nine squares at three times the distance, and sixteen squares at four times the distance, making it look much fainter.*

a bright streak across the dark sky. Lightning is another natural light.

Fire makes natural light, even though most fires are man-made. Some animals make their own light, called "bioluminescence." The best known is the firefly or lightning bug, but there are many others, including a few microscopic animals, some octopuses, and some fish. They get the energy they need from the food they eat. Other natural chemical reactions (called "chemiluminescence") can produce light, but they are very rare.

Some natural light comes from fluorescent or phosphorescent materials that absorb invisible light energy and look eerie in the dark. Fluorescent rocks and man-made materials absorb ultraviolet light, store some of the energy, and quickly release the rest as visible light. Because the ultraviolet light is invisible, it can look like magic, but it is natural. Phosphorescent materials absorb ultraviolet or visible light but store the energy a while before emitting visible light. Usually phosphorescence is fainter than fluorescence, but it lasts longer and shows up even without an ultraviolet light. If you have something that glows in the dark after all your room lights are turned off, it's phosphorescent.

Artificial Light—Beyond Fire

Fear of the dark lies deep in the human soul. Writers set horror stories in the dark. A small child may think that monsters hide in dark corners, but turn on the light and the monsters are gone. We make light to try to drive away the fear and the dark. We are so successful making light that astronomers complain they cannot find the dark they need to see the stars clearly.

For most of history, fire was the only way man knew to make light. Learning to control it constituted progress. Candles and lanterns replaced open fires. In the nineteenth century, natural gas was piped to city homes not for heating and cooking, but for light. Pipes ran through the house to gas fixtures in each room, which were lighted at night. People call the late 1800s the "gaslight era," but gaslights and lanterns lit homes even into the twentieth century. The house where Wilbur and Orville Wright lived in 1903 while building the first airplane was illuminated by gaslight. The brothers believed man could fly, but they weren't that sure about the future of the newfangled electric light bulb. It was only in 1948 that people stopped using a "standard candle" to measure the brightness of light.

Light from a fire or candle may be romantic, but it has serious problems. Fire is inefficient; most of its energy goes into heat. Flames make smoke and soot; hold something that won't burn just over a candle flame, and it soon will be covered with black soot. A fire will die without air, but it must be confined to keep it from spreading. A small accident could let fire escape to cause destruction. Legend blames the great 1871 Chicago fire on Mrs. O'Leary's cow, but if the legend is right, the real culprit was the lantern that the cow kicked over. Even before that time, people were working on better lighting.

Light Bulbs

What we today call the light bulb is a little over a century old, but it was not the first electric light. Scientists in the nineteenth century first made bright light by passing a strong electric current through air in an "electric arc," somewhat like controlled lightning. After they saw that the electric arc was too bright and too short-lived to make a useful lamp, scientists

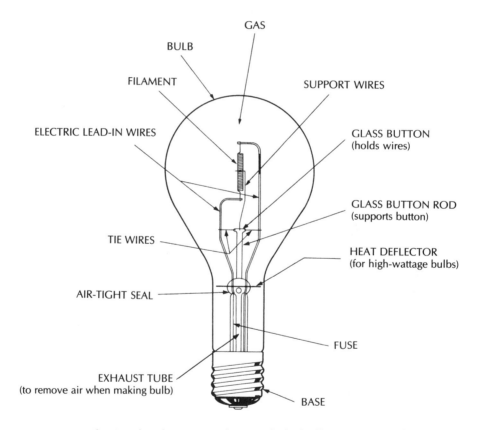

FIGURE 5–2 *The inside of an incandescent light bulb. (Courtesy of GTE Products Corp.)*

had another idea. They heated materials with electricity so they glowed white, or became *incandescent,* and emitted visible light.

That basic science behind an incandescent bulb may be simple, but the practical engineering was not. Most materials will melt or burn long before they reach white heat. Thomas Edison in the United States and Joseph Swan in England tried many materials before they finally found what they needed. Their first incandescent bulbs (invented independently) used thin filaments of carbon sealed inside bulbs from which the air had been removed.

The modern incandescent bulb shown in Figure 5–2 resembles early ones but differs in some important ways. The bulb is filled with an inert gas instead of emptied of all air. The filament is a thin, coiled tungsten wire, suspended from posts within the bulb. Tungsten has replaced carbon because it can be heated almost as hot, is easier to make into the right shape, and is not as brittle. The filament is hidden in most bulbs by a frosting on the inside of the glass, but you can see it in clear bulbs. Shake a clear bulb gently and you will see that the filament is springy. That's because what looks like a wire really is a coil of much thinner wire, wound like a spring. When a bulb "burns out," the filament breaks, and often you can see a loose piece of filament in a burnt-out bulb.

The tungsten filament in a modern bulb reaches about 2600 or 2700 degrees Celsius (a little under 5000 degrees Fahrenheit). That's only about half the temperature of the sun, and that means that the light bulb's peak wavelength is near 10,000 nanometers in the infrared, about twice as long as the sun's. Most of the energy an incandescent bulb emits is in the infrared, which we can feel as heat but can't see, so you could say that an incandescent bulb makes more heat than light.

A bulb's wattage does not tell how much light it emits. It measures only how much electricity it uses. Visible light is measured in *lumens,* which are given on bulb packages. A typical 60-watt incandescent bulb produces 850 to 870 lumens, whereas a 100-watt bulb may produce 1600 to 1800 lumens. Note that the higher-power bulb produces more lumens per watt of power. One 100-watt bulb uses twenty watts less than two 60-watt bulbs but produces about as much light.

Fluorescent and Neon Lights

Fluorescent lights look different from incandescent bulbs. They come in different shapes—long straight tubes or rings. They also produce different types of light, so some colors look different under them.

In a fluorescent tube such as in Figure 5–3, an electric current passes through a gas containing vaporized mercury (a metal that is liquid at room temperature). The mercury atoms take some energy from the current, then emit ultraviolet light, which never gets out of the tube. It strikes a fluorescent coating on the tube that absorbs the ultraviolet light and produces visible light.

The color of light from a fluorescent tube depends on the type of coating. Some coatings produce a blend of colors that looks more natural to the eye than others. If you look through a prism or diffraction grating at a fluorescent tube, you will see a rainbow spectrum, plus colored images of the tube. The colored images are specific wavelengths (called "spectral lines") emitted by the mercury or the coating. Look at an incandescent bulb, and you'll see only a rainbow spectrum.

What happens to the ultraviolet light? Your diffraction grating probably will show one violet line, but most of the ultraviolet is absorbed by the coating or by the tube. You can buy special black light tubes that let

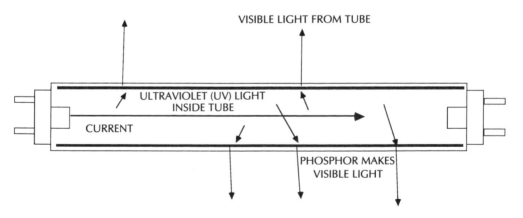

FIGURE 5–3 *Inside a fluorescent tube, showing how the phosphor on the wall of the tube converts ultraviolet light to visible light.*

the ultraviolet light through. They are called black lights because they don't produce any visible light but can make many materials fluoresce.

Starting a fluorescent tube takes a much higher electrical voltage than used in your house, which comes from a "ballast transformer." A fluorescent tube takes a moment to turn on, but once it is on, it is much more efficient than an incandescent bulb. A 40-watt fluorescent tube can produce 2560 lumens, or 64 lumens per watt—more light than a 60- and a 100-watt incandescent bulb combined! Fluorescent tubes also last much longer than incandescent bulbs.

Neon tubes work like fluorescents, but they are filled with neon gas and don't need coatings. When electricity passes through the neon, it emits red-orange light, which passes right through the clear glass tube.

Other Lamps

Fluorescent and incandescent lamps are good for indoor lighing, but other lamps are better elsewhere. Streetlights, for example, must be very bright to light large areas outside. On the other hand, only a tiny bit of light is needed to indicate if your radio is receiving a stereo signal.

Many streetlamps are mercury arc lamps, which look white to your eye. Like fluorescent tubes, they make light by passing a current through mercury vapor, but the conditions inside the streetlamp are different. Look at one through a diffraction grating, and you will see a few sharp colored lines instead of a full rainbow of colors. Those few colors are all the mercury arc emits; they blend together to look white.

Some streetlamps make yellow-orange light. These are low-pressure sodium-vapor lamps, which contain hot vapor of the metal sodium. Look at a low-pressure sodium lamp through a prism or diffraction grating and you won't see a rainbow, only a single yellow-orange stripe, emitted by hot sodium atoms. Sodium is so common that you often see that same color in flames burning something that contains sodium.

That yellow-orange light may be eerie, but low-pressure sodium lamps are very efficient. They also make astronomers happy. Why should astronomers care about streetlamps? Because scattered light from street-lamps makes the sky too bright to see faint stars. Astronomers can get rid of that scattered light if it's only at one wavelength—like the yellow sodium line—but not if it's all through the visible spectrum. When light from San Diego threatened to make the sky too bright at California's famous Mount Palomar Observatory, astronomers convinced city officials to switch to yellow sodium streetlamps.

Tiny Lights

If you have a stereo radio or a digital clock, you probably have seen tiny red lights. They couldn't light up your room, but they tell you the time and whether or not the radio is getting a stereo program.

Light-emitting diodes or LEDs are ideal for indicators and displays. They are semiconductor electronic devices, related to the electronic components in radios and television sets. However, they work differently. When an electric current goes through a light-emitting diode, it produces light. The color depends on the material from which the LED is made. The commonest type is red, but yellow and green LEDs are not unusual. LEDs are not very efficient, but they don't need to make much light, and because they need very little power to work, they can be used in battery-powered electronics.

Lasers

The laser is an artificial light source very different from any lamp. It produces a bright, narrow, single-color beam of light. It can do things far beyond a lamp—but it won't do the job of an ordinary light bulb.

Theodore Maiman fired the world's first laser pulse on May 16, 1960, at Hughes Research Laboratories in Malibu, California. Since then, more nonsense has been written about lasers than about any other optical technology. Lasers are not space-age science-fictional death rays. Military researchers have been trying to make laser weapons for thirty years, but no nation in the world is about to equip its armies with lasers instead of rifles. Laser light does have some special properties, but nothing magical. Laser light can even be produced in nature, although not in the form of a laser beam. And as we will see later, the place you are most likely to find lasers at work is at the checkout counter of your local supermarket.

The road to the laser was not an easy one, but we have the advantage of looking backward. To see what happens inside a laser, we need to look more closely at energy inside atoms and molecules.

Scientists say that atoms or molecules are in energy levels or states, which you can think of as a ladder. Normally, an atom is at the lowest energy level, the ground state at the base of the ladder in Figure 5–4. If the atom gets some extra energy, it is "excited" and can go a step or two up the ladder. Most of the steps on our energy-level ladder are slippery, so the atoms soon slip back down to the ground state. When they slip down, they release as much energy as it took to move them up the steps.

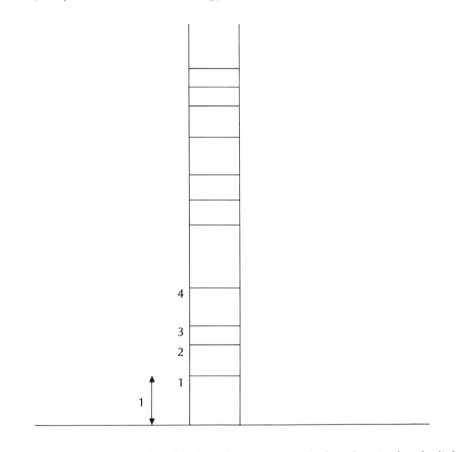

FIGURE 5–4 *The energy-level ladder that an atom climbs when it absorbs light and slips down when it emits light.*

The energy that the atoms gain or lose can be in the form of light. If a 620-nanometer red light moves an atom up from the ground state to level 1, the atom will release a 620-nanometer red photon when it slips back down.

The levels in the energy ladder are fixed, but they are not spaced evenly, as in a real ladder. Each atom and molecule has its own energy-level ladder, so it emits and absorbs light at certain wavelengths—such as the yellow lines of sodium, the red-orange color of a neon tube, or the ultraviolet wavelengths of mercury in a fluorescent tube.

Atoms are excited up the energy ladder in a laser, but they don't slip back down by themselves, as they do in a sodium lamp. Instead, they hang onto one step above the ground until they are pushed or "stimulated" to fall and release light. This is possible because the atom holds onto a step not as slippery as the rest, where it can stay longer. (The scientific term is a *metastable level,* because the atom is almost stable in that state.)

Stimulation is a very important part of what makes a laser work. It works only if the stimulating light has exactly the wavelength produced when the atom slips down that step. Also, many atoms must be perched on that not-very-slippery step. When the right light comes along, it can push them all off, so they all produce light at once, making much more light than you would get if each atom slipped off the step at a different time.

Stimulated emission, as laser light is called, can grow quickly. Suppose that many identical atoms had energy ladders leaning along the wall, and the atoms were all clinging to those sticky steps. If one dropped down and emitted the right wavelength, that light could stimulate another. The light released when that atom slipped down could stimulate others. All the light-stimulated light waves would have exactly the same wavelength, would go in the same direction, and would be in phase with one another, with their peaks and valleys lined up with one another, as in Figure 5–5. Such light is called "coherent."

Many excited atoms are not enough to make what we call a laser. Left by themselves, atoms can emit light in any direction, but we want to collect all the light in a narrow beam. Stimulated light goes in the same

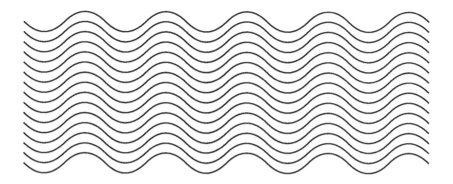

FIGURE 5–5 *These light waves are coherent because all have the same phase and wavelength.*

direction as the light that started it, but starting light could come from any direction.

The best way to get all the light to go in the same direction is to make the laser a long, narrow rod or tube and put a mirror on each end. Light bounces between the mirrors and passes back and forth through the laser, stimulating atoms as it passes. One mirror always lets some light out, which we see as the laser beam.

Theodore Maiman made his first laser by putting a small ruby rod, a few centimeters long, inside a flashlamp shaped like a spring, which he is holding in Figure 5–6. He coated the ends of the rod with metal films to make them act like mirrors. Then he turned on the flashlamp for a split second. Bright light from the flashlamp excited chromium atoms, which give ruby its red color. A few chromium atoms emitted red light right away, and the light bounced back and forth between the mirrors, stimulating more chromium atoms to emit red light and producing the world's first laser pulse. The building up of light within a laser is called amplification, and the whole process by which a laser works is called "light amplification by the stimulated emission of radiation." Take the first letters of the larger words, and you have LASER—which is where the word came from.

The ruby laser was only the first of many types. Like many other solid-state lasers, it is a crystal that contains a few atoms that emit light and many other atoms that hold the light-emitting atoms in place. The

FIGURE 5–6 *Theodore Maiman with the first laser, which he built in 1960. (Courtesy of Theodore Maiman)*

light-emitting atoms get energy from light entering the crystal from outside, usually from a special lamp. Some solid-state lasers are small, like the first one. Others are larger and more powerful. Some make light pulses strong enough to drill holes in diamond or hard metals.

Gas lasers look like fluorescent light tubes, but with mirrors on each end. Like fluorescent tubes, they get their energy from electricity passing through the gas. The type of laser you are most likely to see is a gas laser. It contains a mixture of helium and neon and produces a steady red beam at a wavelength of 633 nanometers. The beam is not powerful enough to cut anything—a few thousandths of a watt or less—and you wouldn't feel it as a warm spot on your skin, but you should never stare directly into it.

Other gas lasers are more powerful. The argon-ion laser emits green light at 514 nanometers and often is used in displays or medicine. Its steady beam is at powers up to about 40 watts. That may not sound like much, but unlike the light from a bulb, it is concentrated in one place. Even more powerful is the carbon-dioxide gas laser, which emits invisible infrared light at a wavelength of 10,600 nanometers—about twenty times longer than visible light. Factories use carbon-dioxide lasers with powers of thousands of watts to cut metals or plastics. A 50-watt surgical carbon-dioxide laser can cut skin.

Most lasers produce light at one fixed wavelength, but not the dye laser. Its wavelength can be changed by adjusting the optics that surround it or by changing the light-emitting dye that is dissolved in a liquid. Dye lasers produce visible light and invisible infrared and ultraviolet light. They are used in scientific research and medicine.

A tiny semiconductor chip also can be a laser. A semiconductor laser makes light somewhat like an LED. However, it works at higher currents and has edges that reflect light and act as mirrors. This lets it produce much more power than an LED. Semiconductor lasers are used in the telephone system and in players of digital compact disk recordings.

Table 5–2 lists the major types of lasers and how they are used. We will talk more about the uses of lasers later.

Natural Lasers

We mentioned earlier that laser action could occur in nature. Natural lasers do not make beams like man-made lasers, but they do amplify stimulated emission. Natural lasers are clouds of gas in space near hot stars. The stars excite molecules in the gas, pushing them up the energy-level ladder, and leaving them ready to be stimulated to emit light. However, they don't really emit light. Their output is microwaves, and they are usually called "cosmic masers," for microwave amplification by stimulated emission.

One of the most surprising facts about cosmic masers is that they were not discovered until 1965, five years after the first laser. So although laser light is not unnatural, people did not discover it in nature until after they had made it in the laboratory.

TABLE 5–2 *Important Lasers and Their Uses*

TYPE	WAVELENGTH	USES
Argon-gas	514 nm (green)	Displays, light shows, printing, medicine
Dye	350–1000 nm	Medicine, research
Helium-neon	633 nm (red)	Supermarket checkout, holography, demonstrations, surveying, etc.
Ruby	693 nm (red)	Drilling, research, holography
Semiconductor	800–900 or longer	Communications, compact disk players
Neodymium	1060 nm	Drilling, research, medicine, measurement
Carbon dioxide	10,600 nm	Cutting, welding, medicine

Light Detection
and Robot Vision

Eyes are good at detecting light, but they can't do everything. If we want to take photographs or television pictures, capture solar energy, or control machinery with light, we need other things called "sensors" or "detectors" because they sense or detect light.

Our eyes work by changing light into impulses that travel along nerves. Most other sensors convert light into electricity. However, a few, such as photographic film, work differently by making light change something that it strikes. In this chapter we will learn how light can be sensed, starting with photography.

Photographic Film and Photochemistry

The basic idea of photography is simple—recording an image. The image must be a real one, usually projected by a positive lens. We use photographic film to record the image.

The active part of photographic film is a compound containing silver and another element (often, but not always, iodine). The atoms are bonded together loosely so that visible light carries enough energy to break them apart, forming metallic silver. The silver compound is light-colored, but the silver powder is black. (The metal looks black rather than shiny because it is made of many tiny particles.) Thus parts of the film exposed to light turn black, and those kept in the dark stay light.

Exposing film in this way makes what is called a "negative" image, where the light areas are dark and the dark areas are light. This looks rather strange, but there's an easy way to turn it back into a positive print, where the light areas are light and the dark areas are dark. Just put the negative on top of another piece of film, and expose the film with light. The dark parts of the negative will block light, so the places underneath them will be light. The light parts of the negative will let light through, so the areas under them will become dark. The result looks like the original scene, as shown in Figure 6–1.

Photography isn't really that simple. We have to look at photographs in the light. If a photograph were still sensitive to light, taking it out to look at it would make the whole thing turn dark. No image would be left at all. To prevent that, film developers get rid of the silver compound so it can't break down to form black silver. They put the film into water containing the compound sodium hyposulfite, or "hypo," which dissolves the silver compound. All developing must be done without exposing the film to light, so photographers work in a special darkroom.

The films we have described so far produce only black-and-white photos. Color films are more complex. They contain separate layers sensitive to red, green, and blue. Each layer contains a colored dye, which shows up when the film is exposed, instead of the black silver in a black-and-white film. Some color films are made to produce negatives and prints. Others—used in color slides or "instant" cameras—have different dyes and reproduce images showing the scene without an intermediate negative.

Color photography is tricky. Carefully compare color prints and slides with the real world, and you may notice that all the colors are not perfect. That's because three dyes cannot exactly copy all the colors in the spectrum. In good films, the differences are hard to see, but a professional photographer can notice them. Also, some dyes fade with age, causing colors to change with time and making some old color pictures look strange.

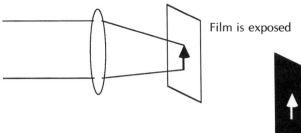 Film is exposed

to produce a negative

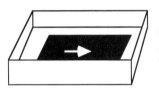 Negative is developed
and fixed so it doesn't
turn all black

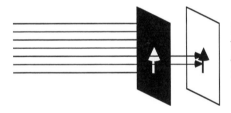 Light rays passing through
the negative expose
a positive image to
make the final photograph

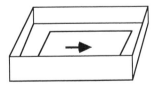 The positive is fixed
and developed

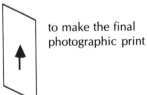 to make the final
photographic print

FIGURE 6–1 *Stages in making a photograph.*

Photographic processing is an example of photochemistry, the use of light to cause a chemical reaction. In this case, the chemical reaction forms silver from the original silver compounds. You sometimes see other kinds of photochemical reactions without knowing what they are. For example, red plastics tend to lose their color in the sun. The reason is that sunlight breaks down the compounds that color the plastics red. Thus, in a way, the change in color "senses" how much sunlight reaches the plastic.

Copying Machines

Although they are often called "photocopiers," copying machines do not use photographic film. They work by an entirely different process, in which an image of a page is focused onto a rotating drum coated with a light-sensitive material. The basic idea is shown in Figure 6–2.

The key to the process is the coating on the drum. Normally, the coating can hold an electric charge, because it does not conduct electricity. However, light makes the coating conduct electricity, so the charge on the surface goes away.

Starting the copier charges the whole drum coating and turns on a bright light, which shines on the original. Lenses focus an image of the original onto the drum. Where no light reaches the coating, the drum holds the charge. However, where light falls on the surface, the charge is released. Thus, the coating saves an image of the original page as a pattern of charged and uncharged areas.

Our eyes cannot see electric charge, but engineers can make the pattern of charges visible. They add tiny particles of a black (or other dark-colored) *toner* to the drum. The particles stick to the charged areas (the dark spots of the original) but not to the uncharged area (the light parts of the original). Then that pattern of particles is transferred to paper, a copy of the original. The process of transferring the toner to the paper is tricky, and sometimes it does not stick well—which is why the black sometimes smudges on photocopies. Photocopies are not as sharp as photographs because the process is not as precise.

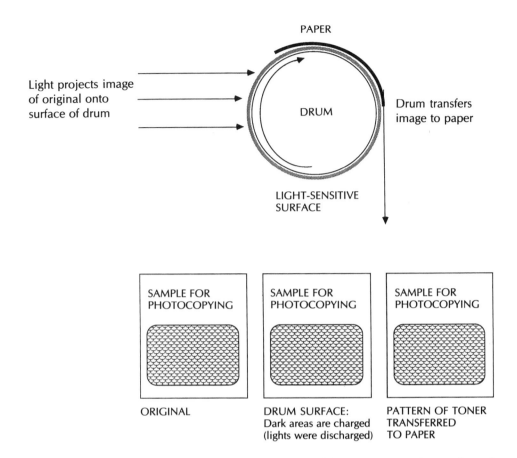

PAPER

Light projects image of original onto surface of drum

DRUM

Drum transfers image to paper

LIGHT-SENSITIVE SURFACE

| SAMPLE FOR PHOTOCOPYING | SAMPLE FOR PHOTOCOPYING | SAMPLE FOR PHOTOCOPYING |
| ORIGINAL | DRUM SURFACE: Dark areas are charged (lights were discharged) | PATTERN OF TONER TRANSFERRED TO PAPER |

FIGURE 6–2 *In a copying machine light reflected from an original (not shown) forms an image on a light-sensitive drum, and that image is transferred to paper to make a copy.*

Solar Cells and Electronic Detectors

Photographic film and photocopiers detect light to record images or patterns. We also need to detect light to control machines and transmit television images. To do those jobs, we first must convert light into electricity.

The most direct way to change light into electricity is with a solar cell. A solar cell is a piece of semiconductor divided into two parts in which electricity flows differently because they each contain small amounts of different materials. One part contains materials that release extra electrons, which can carry current. The other contains materials that soak up extra electrons, creating "holes" where electrons should be. In a sense, those holes can also carry current, but really they don't. The holes seem to move because electrons move to fill them and leave holes behind elsewhere.

We saw earlier that light carries energy. Atoms in the solar cell absorb that light energy. If that energy is large enough—that is, if the wavelength is short enough—the energy can free an electron from the semiconductor material, leaving behind a hole, as shown in Figure 6–3. Both can carry current. If the light is bright enough to produce many current carriers, the solar cell generates electrical energy. Shine enough light on a large enough area, and solar cells can deliver enough elec-

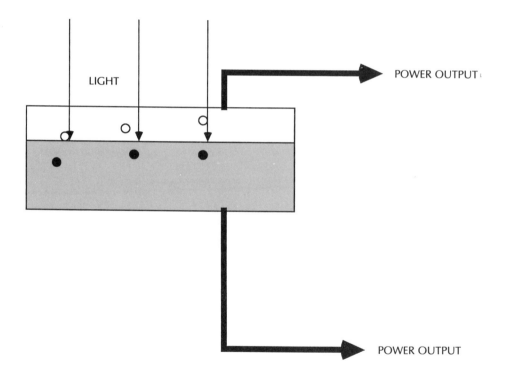

FIGURE 6–3 *Light striking the junction between the two parts of a solar cell frees electrons and holes, generating electrical power and making a current flow.*

tricity to make something work. One example is a solar-powered calculator.

Solar cells are not very efficient; the best convert 20 percent of the light energy they receive to electricity, and ordinary ones convert less. They can power a calculator, which doesn't require much energy, but a roof full of them couldn't operate your refrigerator. Solar cells are used mostly for making electric power, but similar devices are often used to detect light.

Simple Electronic Detectors

The more light that hits a solar cell, the more electrons and holes can carry current, and the stronger the current that flows from it. That means that if you measure the current from a solar cell, you can tell about how much light is hitting it. However, solar cells are made to generate energy, and trying to use them to measure light is like trying to tell time with a clock having no minute hand. You can tell about how much light there is, but you can't tell very well.

To measure light accurately, you need a different type of semiconductor device made to measure light. It is used in a different type of circuit and called a "detector" or "photodiode." You need not worry about the differences unless you are trying to build something.

A detector, sometimes called an "electronic eye," can control a machine. For example it can look to see if an elevator door can be closed, as in Figure 6–4. On one side of the door is a lamp that emits invisible infrared light. The detector is on the other. When the elevator comes to a floor, the door opens and waits long enough for people to get out. Then the electronic eye looks for the infrared light. If a person or a package is in the way, the light cannot get through, telling the door not to close. If nothing is in the way, the door will try to close. (Elevator doors also stop closing if they hit anything.)

Simple electronic sensors can do other jobs. Many cameras have sensors to measure how bright a scene is. Other electronics in the camera use that measurement to adjust the exposure, so the photo is not too light or too dark.

Many streetlamps are controlled by light sensors, which turn the

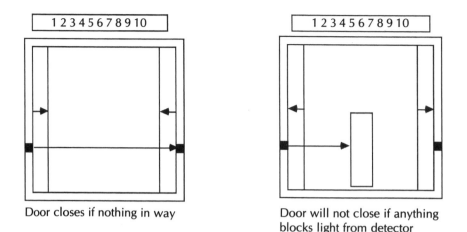

| 1 2 3 4 5 6 7 8 9 10 | 1 2 3 4 5 6 7 8 9 10 |

Door closes if nothing in way

Door will not close if anything blocks light from detector

FIGURE 6–4 *A detector controls an elevator door by looking for light from the other side. If light reaches the detector, nothing is in the way, and the door can close. Otherwise it stays open.*

lamp on when it starts getting dark. If it gets very dark during the day, as can happen when there are heavy clouds, the light might come on. If a bright light—like a car headlight—shines on the sensor at night, the light might go out. (The lamp waits a while before switching on or off, to make sure the light is not just from a passing car.)

IMAGE SENSORS AND TELEVISION CAMERAS

So far we have talked only about sensors that look at or measure the total light. The elevator sensor just looks to see if light is present. The camera sensor measures the total amount of light. That can be useful, but sometimes it isn't enough. Suppose you want to know who is in the elevator. It isn't enough just to know that someone is inside. You need to see his or her face. That's one example of when you need an image sensor, which can detect a pattern of light.

We saw earlier how photographic film and copiers can record a pattern. Special electronic sensors also can record patterns.

One way to sense an image electronically is to put together many separate sensors in an array, as shown in Figure 6–5. That array is five elements wide and five high, so it is called a "five by five array," and contains twenty-five detector cells. Such an array can see a simple image, such as the letter T shown, but it is not good for seeing patterns with

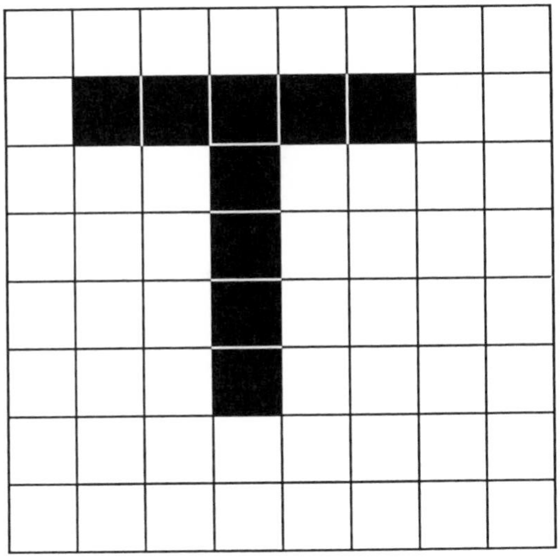

FIGURE 6–5 *An array sensor, with the letter T projected onto it.*

finer details, such as faces. To see a face properly, an array must have many more elements on each side. The more elements an array has, the harder it is to make. The problems come not just in putting the tiny detectors together, but in making sure the electronic signals they produce don't get mixed up.

A few television cameras work like that, using arrays of sensors with a hundred or more elements on a side. However, most television cameras work differently. Optics in the camera project light onto a screen coated with a special material that becomes charged electrically when light strikes it. (This is the opposite of a copying machine, where light discharges the coating.) A beam of electrons scans regularly across the surface of the screen, to read how much charge has accumulated at each point on the surface. That beam of electrons makes the electronic signal, which is recorded and ultimately makes the image you see on your television screen.

Television cameras scan their screens in a standard way, so the picture will look the same on all television sets. Look carefully at a television screen, and you can see that the picture is made up of many thin lines, each made by one scan of the electron beam across the sensing screen, as shown in Figure 6–6. In the United States, Canada, Mexico, Japan, and some other countries standard cameras scan 525 lines on a

FIGURE 6-6 *In many television cameras, an electron beam scans across a screen that becomes charged when exposed to light. The beam picks up the pattern of charges to generate a television signal. Actual television cameras scan many more lines than shown.*

full screen thirty times a second. (Television standards are different in Europe, where 625-line screens are scanned twenty-five times a second.)

Robot Vision

At the start of this chapter, we mentioned robot vision but haven't said a word about robots since. However, we have been talking about robot vision, because robots see with electronic sensor eyes.

Real-world robots are not science-fictional metal people, just machines that do things automatically. Our elevator door operator is a simple robot, which opens when it comes to a floor and closes automatically, checking to make sure no one remains in the doorway.

The elevator door operator is a very simple robot; it does only one job, moving a door back and forth. More complex robots do other jobs in factories. A robot hand might reach into a box to get a part to lay on a moving belt.

Some robots work by feel. For example, the part-picking robot might have a "hand" shaped so it could pick up the part only one way, the right way to lay it on the moving belt. However, other robots need to "see."

Suppose you need a robot cart to pick up a heavy block of metal and move it to another place in a factory. You could have the machine that makes the metal block always put it in the same place and have the robot always pick it up at the same angle. However, if that was all the robot did, it would not stop if something or someone was in its way. If you added a light sensor, the robot could look ahead and stop if it saw anything in the way. This would keep it from crashing into people or things accidentally put into its path.

Robots with harder jobs need to know more than whether or not anything is in the way. Suppose a robot had to get screws from a box containing other parts. It would be nice if the robot could tell the screws from other parts. A simple detector wouldn't help because it can tell only the total amount of light. The robot needs to ''see'' an image of the inside of the box.

Robots do not see as people do. They are programmed to know certain patterns. Suppose a robot's job is to pick the letter **T** from the twenty-six capital letters of the alphabet. To make the robot's job simple, we will make the letters all black, the same size, and standing straight up on a white shelf. And we won't put anything else on the shelf, so the robot won't be confused by other things. Our robot's eye is an array of twenty-five sensing elements, five across and five long.

Figure 6–7 shows how the **T** would look to the robot's sensing eye. When the robot looks at a letter, it compares what its eye sees to what it would see if it were looking at a **T.** If all the cells that should be black are black, and all the cells that should be white are white, the letter is a **T.** If any do not match, the letter is not a **T.** For example, if the middle line is there, but not the top, the robot ignores it. If the top bar is there, but not the upright, the letter is not a **T** and the robot ignores it. If we programmed the robot more, it could recognize other letters, using patterns such as those shown in Figure 6–7 for an **I, F, Z,** and **B.**

We gave our robot a very simple job. All the letters were the same size. If the **T** had been smaller, so it didn't fill all the boxes, our robot would not know it was a **T.** If the **T** were on its side or turned sideways, the robot would not know it was a **T.** If the background and letters were the same color, the robot's eye would have seen the same amount of light from each cell and not seen any letters at all.

The real world is not as kind to robots as we were. Suppose we wanted to make a robot deer hunter. The robot would have to know what a deer looked like from one or fifty meters away. It would have to know what a deer looked like from the front, the side, and the tail. It would have to spot a brown deer in the brown woods. It would have to spot a deer when only its head was peering out from behind a tree. And it would have to know that cows, sheep, and goats were not deer.

Robots can't do that job yet, because they can't see that well. The problem is not just their light sensors. Like human vision, robot vision depends on the brain as well as the eye. Even if the image of a deer showed on the robot's sensor, the robot's brain would have to recognize the image as a deer. Scientists call that "pattern recognition," and that's the hardest part of the job.

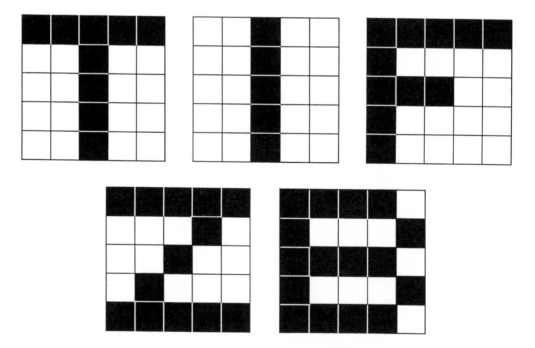

FIGURE 6–7 *How several letters would appear to a robot "eye" made up of an array of five by five sensors. The robot can be programmed to know what each pattern means.*

People and animals are good at recognizing patterns and knowing what the patterns mean. That is the outcome of hundreds of millions of years of evolution. Animals must recognize things in order to survive. They have to find food and avoid other animals that might eat them. A rabbit must know what it can eat and be on the lookout for foxes that might eat it. Foxes, in turn, must be able to find rabbits and other small animals to eat. You could say that animal brains are wired for pattern recognition.

Robot brains are wired differently. Electronic computers are very good at arithmetic, but pattern recognition is not arithmetic. Scientists are studying ways that light might be used to help in pattern recognition, in what are called "optical computers," but that's a future story that we will save for the last chapter.

Invisible Light:
The Infrared
and the Ultraviolet

Earlier we saw how visible light was part of the large family of electromagnetic waves. Some members of that family are quite different from light, but the two closest relatives—infrared and ultraviolet light—behave very much like visible light. Many sensors can see them, and they can do many useful things. The main difference between them and visible light is that they are invisible to the human eye. If you look closely, even that borderline isn't a sharp one because our vision fades gradually into the infrared and ultraviolet.

The Limits of Visibility

In Chapter 2, we said visible light has wavelengths between 400 nanometers (violet) and 700 nanometers (red). Those are useful borders but not rigid ones. Light does not suddenly become invisible when you go beyond 400 or 700 nanometers. I have looked into instruments that let you change the wavelength of light, and as you turn wavelength slowly beyond those borders, the light is not turned off. It fades away. It's like listening to a faint sound in a quiet room. Turn the sound lower and lower and it fades away. At some point, you can't hear it anymore—but it is very hard to be sure when you stopped hearing it.

Different things cut off your vision at short and long wavelengths. The lens of the eye limits your ultraviolet vision because it absorbs ultraviolet light before it can reach the retina. Other parts of the eye absorb shorter ultraviolet wavelengths. This is not an accident. It helps to protect your eye because too much ultraviolet light could damage your vision if it reaches your retina.

Light at wavelengths longer than the red end of the visible spectrum does reach the retina. However, we can't see it because the pigments in the retina do not respond to it. You can see farther into the infrared than into the ultraviolet because the cones do respond very weakly to longer wavelengths, but don't expect any mysteries to be revealed if you peer into the fringes of the infrared. The light you see looks like ordinary red light, and it just gets fainter and fainter as wavelength increases, until you realize the color isn't there at all.

The Infrared

Because people can't see infrared light, it was not discovered until the end of the 1700s. British scientist Sir William Herschel was measuring heat in different colors of light. He spread out the spectrum with a prism and put thermometers at different points. He found that red was the "hottest" color, then decided to put a thermometer beyond the red, as shown in Figure 7–1. He found that it was warm there, too, and realized that he had detected invisible light. (The word infrared, which came later, means *below* red on the wavelength scale.)

Some people call infrared light "heat radiation." As we saw earlier, infrared light is not really heat, but it is a form of energy that hot bodies give off. The sun is hot enough that most of its energy is emitted as visible light, but stoves, heaters, and radiators are cooler and give off most of their energy as infrared light. Everything at ordinary temperatures also emits some infrared radiation, with wavelength centered near 10,000 nanometers.

We also think of infrared light as "heat radiation" because our skins absorb most of it. Human skin, no matter what its color in visible light,

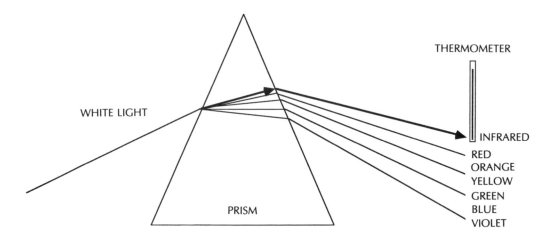

FIGURE 7–1 *Infrared light was discovered when Sir William Herschel put a thermometer beyond the red end of the visible spectrum and found the invisible light heated it.*

absorbs more than 90 percent of infrared light at wavelengths longer than 1500 nanometers. That high absorption helps give you the warm feeling you get from sunlight or an infrared heater.

THE INFRARED WORLD

The range of infrared wavelengths is much larger than the visible part of the electromagnetic spectrum. The infrared runs from the edge of the visible, at 700 nanometers, to the edge of the microwave region, at 1,000,000 nanometers. To understand just how big that is, let's borrow a term from music—the octave. Two notes are an octave apart if one has twice the frequency of the other. The visible spectrum is almost one octave wide. The infrared spans more than ten octaves.

How would the world look to infrared eyes? The infrared is so big that it depends on what part we might be seeing. In the "near infrared," close to the visible, most things would look about as bright or dark as they are in visible light. (We can't guess what infrared colors would look like, so we'll look at the infrared world in black and white.) Green plants are an exception, because they reflect near-infrared light strongly and would be very bright to infrared eyes. So would some types of sand and soil.

The world would look stranger at longer wavelengths. Snow and water would be black, because water absorbs strongly in the infrared. So would plants and animals (because of the water they contain). Even the air would be murky, because infrared light cannot travel as far through air as can visible light.

You would see a strange world indeed if your eyes could sense the 10,000 nanometer light that objects emit at ordinary temperatures. The whole world would glow in its own light. Warm-blooded animals would be brighter than plants or buildings, because they are warmer. If you were barefoot, you could see if your toes were cold because they would not be as bright as warmer parts of your body.

THE GREENHOUSE EFFECT

The world would look strange to our "infrared eyes" because air and other things about us react differently to infrared light than to visible light. Some of these differences are useful for things like heating a greenhouse on a sunny, cold winter day, as shown in Figure 7–2.

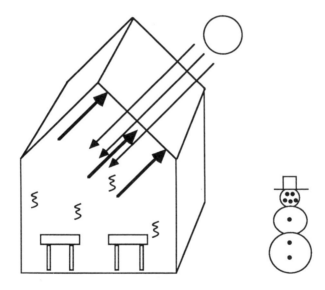

FIGURE 7–2 *Glass in a greenhouse lets visible light through but does not transmit infrared light. Things inside the greenhouse absorb the visible light and release energy as infrared light, which can't get out and stays inside to help heat the greenhouse.*

Glass lets visible sunlight into the greenhouse, and the energy from the sunlight heats the building, just as it warms you if you lie in the sun. Plants and other things inside the greenhouse absorb the solar energy, then release it as infrared light. However, the glass keeps the infrared light from getting out of the greenhouse, trapping the sun's energy and warming the greenhouse. (The glass also traps warm air so it can't mix with the cold outside air, and usually greenhouses also have heaters to keep them warm on cloudy days.) This is called the "greenhouse effect," but you don't need a greenhouse to feel it. It works on a bright winter day for a room with plenty of windows facing the sun—but the room gets cooler once the sun sets.

The greenhouse effect can warm a whole planet. Carbon dioxide and water vapor in the air transmit visible light but absorb infrared light. They work like the glass on a greenhouse to trap the sun's energy during the daytime. Less than 1 percent of the air is water vapor and carbon dioxide, but they do help keep the earth warmer than it would be without them. The planet Venus has much more carbon dioxide in its atmosphere, and the greenhouse effect heats it to temperatures of 475 degrees Celsius (nearly 900 degrees Fahrenheit).

Burning wood, oil, gas, and coal adds more carbon dioxide to the air. Some scientists worry that this extra carbon dioxide could add to the greenhouse effect and warm the earth enough to melt the polar icecaps, raising sea level and changing climate. However, we are not sure how much carbon dioxide would be needed to cause a problem.

THE INFRARED AT WORK

Infrared light helps in many types of heating. Scientists talk of three types of heating: conductive, convective, and radiational. All three work together.

Conductive heating occurs when heat goes directly or is conducted from a warm object to a cold one. For example, the heat that warms a pan of water on a stove is conducted through the stove and the pan to the water.

Convective heating is by air currents, which pick up warmth and distribute it. A warm breeze is one example. Another is when you blow your warm breath on your cold hands in the winter. Because warm air is lighter than cold air, the rising of warm air can generate its own air currents.

Radiative heating is the radiation of infrared light. If you hold your hands near a red-hot electric heater or stove burner, your hands absorb infrared light and feel warm. Actually, you can be warmed by convective heating through the air as well (and if you touched the heater, conductive heating would burn you!).

Other uses of infrared light have little to do with energy or heating. Many optical sensors, like the one in the robot elevator door we talked about in the last chapter, look for infrared light rather than visible light. In Chapter 10, we will learn how infrared light can carry information through the air or through long fibers of glass.

Many of the most powerful lasers produce infrared rather than visible light. Engineers can use those powerful beams of infrared light to drill holes or cut plastic or metal. Infrared laser beams also can replace knives in some types of surgery.

Ultraviolet Light

The name *ultraviolet* means beyond violet, because the ultraviolet lies beyond the violet end of the visible spectrum. The ultraviolet wavelengths nearest visible light, like those in the infrared, behave much like visible light, while those farther from the visible behave quite differently.

The ultraviolet range is large, but not as large as the infrared if we use the same "octave" units. The ultraviolet starts at 400 nanometers and extends about five octaves to 10 nanometers. Much of the ultraviolet is not well explored. There are few good sources of wavelengths shorter than 100 nanometers. Another problem is air, which blocks ultraviolet wavelengths shorter than 200 nanometers. (Scientists often call wavelengths of 10 to 200 nanometers the "vacuum ultraviolet," because they can study it only in a vacuum, with no air present.)

The air keeps most of the sun's ultraviolet light from reaching the earth, and that is a good thing because too much ultraviolet light can be dangerous. One important gas that absorbs ultraviolet light high in the atmosphere is ozone, a molecule that contains three oxygen atoms. Scientists are concerned that some types of air pollution might destroy the protective ozone layer.

We can't "see" ultraviolet light directly, but we can see it make some things glow or fluoresce. Special fluorescent paints or crayons and certain rocks absorb invisible ultraviolet light, then release part of that energy as visible light. Fluorescent paint lit only by an ultraviolet light seems to glow in the dark (although the invisible ultraviolet light really is illuminating it).

THE ULTRAVIOLET WORLD

Just into the ultraviolet, the world would look much the same as we see at visible wavelengths (except, of course, the colors). Differences would become more obvious at shorter wavelengths.

One important difference is that the ultraviolet world would look darker, even at wavelengths not far from the visible. Caucasian or "white" human skin reflects 35 percent of all sunlight reaching it, but only 1 percent of the sun's ultraviolet rays. A sandy grass area reflects 17 percent of all sunlight, but only 2.5 percent of the sun's ultraviolet rays. Even ordinary glass absorbs ultraviolet light strongly, although some special glasses can transmit some ultraviolet light.

At shorter wavelengths, the ultraviolet world would grow darker and eventually black. It would be like being in a thick fog on a moonless night even at noon, because the air soaks up the sun's short ultraviolet rays. If you had ultraviolet eyes sensitive at 100 nanometers, you wouldn't see anything. The air itself would be black.

SUNTAN AND SUNBURN

Ultraviolet photons have more energy than visible light (and much more energy than infrared photons). They have enough to affect the structures of many molecules, causing damage that can have serious side effects on you and other living things. The shorter the wavelength, the higher the energy and the worse the possible damage.

Your skin is the part of your body that gets the most ultraviolet light. Ultraviolet rays cause both suntan and sunburn. We may joke that a suntan and a sunburn are just different degrees of "cooking," but they are different.

A suntan is nature's way of protecting your skin from too much ultraviolet light. When you sit outside on a sunny day, ultraviolet light sinks into your skin and causes slight chemical changes in molecules in your cells. Scientists do not know all the changes, but they do know that in several days the cells start making more of a dark pigment called "melanin." The more melanin in your skin, the darker it is. The melanin apparently absorbs or scatters the ultraviolet light before it can damage other parts of the cell.

Melanin is the pigment that makes skin dark. People differ both in the usual level of melanin in their skin and in their ability to make the pigment. Blacks, whose ancestors lived in tropical Africa for thousands of generations, have much more than whites, whose ancestors were not exposed to as much sunlight. You can see the difference among Europeans. Italians, who come from the southern part of the continent, tend to be darker than Swedes, who live much farther north. However, all people with the same racial background do not have the same coloring.

Exposure to some sunlight is healthy, but not if you overdo it, especially if you are fair-skinned. Too much ultraviolet light can damage some molecules in the skin. You don't feel the damage right away, but within a few hours, you find you are sunburned. The redness and soreness you feel are not caused by the sunlight itself but by the body's natural defenses trying to repair the damage.

Sunburn is short-term damage from too much ultraviolet light on one day. People who stay out in the bright sun continually without protection can do even more damage to their skin. The skin may age rapidly. Teenagers who spend all summer on the beach getting a deep tan are likely to be staring at wrinkles in the mirror in their thirties. Worse yet, too much ultraviolet light can damage DNA, the genetic material in your cells, and cause skin cancer.

There are easy ways to prevent this damage and still enjoy the sun. Many people use sun blockers, lotions that cover your skin and block most of the ultraviolet rays. Sitting behind glass also prevents sunburn because glass doesn't transmit the damaging short-wavelength ultraviolet rays.

All this happens with ultraviolet light at wavelengths longer than 300 nanometers. Shorter-wavelength ultraviolet light could cause sunburn and other problems if it reached your skin, but the air absorbs most of what the sun emits before it can reach the surface of the earth.

THE ULTRAVIOLET AT WORK

The photochemical changes caused by ultraviolet light are not all bad. They can be useful in "curing" plastics, turning liquids quickly into solids. They also can speed some photographic and photocopying processes.

Suppose you want to coat something—a fiber, for example—with a protective plastic layer. To make it easy to apply the plastic, the coating material should be liquid, but if the coating is to be useful, it should be tough. Some plastics are liquid when hot and hard when cool, but many aren't. One way to solve the problem is to coat the fiber with a liquid plastic, then change the plastic chemically. This can be done by shining a bright ultraviolet light onto the liquid coating. The light "cures" the plastic, making a hard, durable layer.

That's one example of photochemistry. In the last chapter, we talked about another, photography. You can make photographs with ultraviolet as well as visible light. Why bother with ultraviolet? You wouldn't bother if you were taking ordinary photographs, but there are times when ultraviolet light can work better. The master "plates" from which newspapers are printed, for instance, are made with a photographic process, similar to making a print from a negative. If the plate is sensitive to visible light, it must be used in the dark. Plates sensitive to the ultraviolet but not to visible light can be used in the light.

The Rest of the Electromagnetic Spectrum

We said earlier that there are other types of electromagnetic waves besides visible, infrared, and ultraviolet light. We showed them in Figure 1–2. X rays have shorter wavelengths than ultraviolet light, and gamma rays even shorter wavelengths. On the other end of the spectrum are microwaves and radio waves. All are members of the same family, but they do not behave alike. Because they are not really "optical," they are not within the scope of this book.

You should realize that the borderlines between types of electromagnetic waves often are hazy. Scientists discovered them one at a time, not realizing that they all went together. For example, infrared and radio waves were discovered at different times by different people. At the time they seemed separate, but they were only as separate as islands in a flooded stream. When the dark waters between them went down, scientists found that the two "islands" were part of the same land. Today they still have a hard time deciding on a dividing line between them.

Seeing Better:
Optical Instruments

For hundreds of years, the main purpose for optics was to help people see better. It started some 700 years ago with the first eyeglasses. Telescopes, binoculars, and microscopes followed, to make things look larger and closer.

All are important. Many of us would be helpless without eyeglasses or contact lenses. (I am so nearsighted I can only see clearly about ten centimeters, or four inches, past the tip of my nose.) At night, a telescope will let you see stars and details of the sky that your eye could never see by itself. Binoculars will bring a wild animal much closer to you than the animal would let you come. A microscope will let you see tiny creatures invisible to the naked eye.

We call these objects optical instruments. They are made of lenses (and sometimes of mirrors), the simple optical elements we learned about in Chapter 3. To see how they work, we will take a short trip through history and find out how people made the first optical instruments.

Eyeglasses

The ancients knew something of lenses and mirrors, but the idea of eyeglasses apparently eluded them. We do not know who made the first eyeglasses, but we believe they were made in the late 1200s in Italy. The first recorded mention of eyeglasses occurs in a sermon given in 1306 by Friar Giordano, a priest in Pisa, Italy:

> It is not twenty years since there was found the art of making eyeglasses which make for good vision, one of the best arts and most necessary that the world has. So short a time it is since there was invented a new art that never existed. I have seen the man who first invented and created it, and I have talked to him.

From the tone of his words, we can guess that Friar Giordano probably wore glasses himself. The invention was an important one, even though those first eyeglasses corrected only the farsightedness that comes as the lens of the eye hardens with age. Without glasses, that farsightedness could keep older people from reading, and few fates are worse for aging scholars. Alas, Friar Giordano did not record the name of the inventor, and it is lost to history.

Eyeglass-making soon became an important trade, its secrets jealously guarded by craftsmen. The rich and powerful would pay well to preserve their vision, so a good spectacle maker could live well if he guarded his secrets from competitors.

The lenses in early eyeglasses would not be good enough for use today, but the quality was remarkable for the technology of the time. The oldest known eyeglasses with lenses, dating from about 1320, are shown in Figure 8–1. They were found in 1953 in the Wienhausen Convent near Celle on the Luneberg Heath in West Germany. A rivet in the middle of the wooden frame let the wearer adjust the two pieces to fit over the nose.

The Birth of the Telescope

Three hundred years passed before the art of the eyeglass-maker gave birth to the telescope. Apparently it was an accidental discovery. The

FIGURE 8–1 *The oldest known spectacles, made about 1320, were found in 1953 in the Wienhausen Convent in West Germany (From Hort Appuhn, Zeiss Werkzeitschrift, Oberkochen, 6, 2, 1958, No. 27, Photo by Hans Grubenbecher; courtesy of Carl Zeiss Optical Museum, Oberkochen, West Germany)*

story has it that in about 1600 two children were playing with lenses in the shop of Hans Lippershey, a spectacle-maker in the Dutch town of Middelburg. They lined up two lenses, looked through them, and were surprised to see the weathervane on the town church much magnified. The excited children told Lippershey, who looked for himself. A practical man, Lippershey soon began making and selling telescopes.

The time was ripe for telescopes, and it was not long before many other spectacle-makers were building them—and claiming the invention for themselves. In 1608, Lippershey asked the Dutch government to give him a patent on the telescope and make the invention a state secret, but his request was denied. In 1609, telescopes were being sold in Paris. In 1610, one came into the hands of Galileo Galilei, an Italian scientist who turned it to the sky and revolutionized astronomy and our view of the universe.

Galileo's telescope was crude by modern standards, but it showed him things that no one else had seen before. He saw four tiny stars that stayed in a line near the planet Jupiter, each night moving to new positions. These, he realized, were moons that circled Jupiter. That was an astounding idea at a time when most people thought that the sun, the planets, the moon, and the stars all circled the earth. Galileo used it as evidence that the earth circled the sun and wound up arrested by order of the Pope.

It is hard to realize now, when even walking on the moon is history, how much change the telescope wrought in our view of the sky. Galileo's visions were only the first. His telescope was too poor to show him the rings of Saturn. Instrument makers built bigger and better telescopes. Discovery followed discovery, and still efforts continue to build bigger telescopes on the ground and even in space.

Scientific advances over the past half-century have opened other parts of the spectrum to astronomers. They can learn about stars and galaxies by looking at X rays and radio waves, but they still think of the sky as something you see. They call their new instruments radio telescopes and X-ray telescopes; they take the numbers that come from them to plot pictures of how the sky would look to X-ray or radio eyes.

The telescope has come a long way since Galileo's time. The type Galileo used, now called the Galilean telescope, is made from two lenses, one positive and one negative, as shown in Figure 8–2. The positive lens must have a long focal length, and the negative lens must

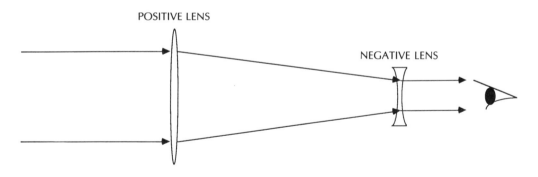

FIGURE 8–2 *A Galilean telescope uses a positive lens to focus light and a negative lens for viewing. (The lens closest to the eye is called the "eyepiece.") It does not magnify much, but it let Galileo discover the moons of Jupiter.*

be between the positive lens and its focal point. The magnification depends on the focal length of the positive lens and the position of the negative lens, so you can change how large things look by moving the lens closest to the eye. This design does not allow large magnification, but to Galileo any magnification was better than the unaided eye. Today it is used rarely, in inexpensive toy telescopes and in opera glasses, in which two Galilean telescopes are mounted side by side so you can see through both eyes. Its main advantage today is that the image is right-side up.

Replacing the negative lens near the eye with a positive lens gave a more powerful telescope, although at the cost of turning the image upside down. The idea came from German astronomer Johannes Kepler, and this sort of telescope, shown in Figure 8–3, is often called a Keplerian telescope in his honor. This design is used in most refracting telescopes, so-called because they focus light by refraction. The large, light-collecting lens has a long focal length. The lens near the eye has a much shorter focal length. In practice, the lens near the eye is often replaced by an assembly of two or more lenses to improve the telescope's optical quality.

Large lenses with long focal lengths are hard to make, so astronomers soon found another alternative: the reflecting telescope, which collects light with a concave mirror. Like a positive lens, a concave mirror

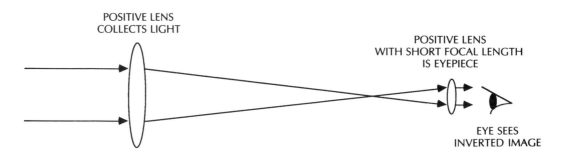

FIGURE 8–3 *A Keplerian refracting telescope collects light with a long-focal-length positive lens. The eye looks through a positive lens with short focal length to see an inverted image. This design is still used in refracting telescopes, although two or more lenses often are put together to serve as an eyepiece, and the focusing lens typically is achromatic.*

can focus light to make a real image. Like a refracting telescope, a reflecting telescope uses a short-focal-length positive lens as an eyepiece to look through. It, too, inverts the image.

If you put the eyepiece near the focal point of the mirror in a reflecting telescope, your head would keep light from reaching it. To avoid that problem, the great British scientist Sir Isaac Newton designed a reflecting telescope with a small, flat mirror near the focal point of the large concave mirror. This reflected the light out to the side of a tube, where you can look at it without your head getting in the way of the incoming light,

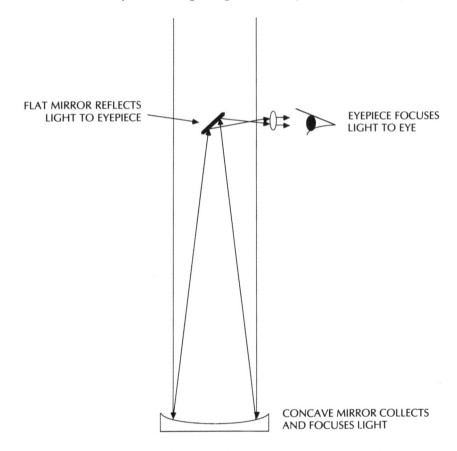

FLAT MIRROR REFLECTS
LIGHT TO EYEPIECE

EYEPIECE FOCUSES
LIGHT TO EYE

CONCAVE MIRROR COLLECTS
AND FOCUSES LIGHT

FIGURE 8–4 *The Newtonian reflecting telescope uses a concave mirror to collect light and focus it toward the eyepiece. A flat mirror reflects light to the side, so you can look through the telescope without your head blocking the light.*

as shown in Figure 8–4. Since Newton's time, many other variations on the reflecting telescope have been developed, far too many to show here.

Binoculars

One of the first questions Hans Lippershey was asked about the telescope was: can you make one that will let people see through both eyes? That is the idea behind binoculars, a word that comes from *bi* (which means two) and *ocular* (which means eyepiece). Binoculars are made of two telescopes, mounted together so one eye looks through each and aligned so each eye sees the same scene. Cheap binoculars, such as you might find in a toy store, are a pair of Galilean telescopes. Often called opera glasses or field glasses, they are limited in magnification and optical quality, but they are cheap to make.

"Real" binoculars are more complex and expensive but give you a better view of the world. They actually are miniature Keplerian refracting telescopes, with internal prisms that flip the image so it appears right-side-up and shorten the tube's length to make binoculars easier to handle.

If you ever try to buy prism binoculars, you will find that they come in several types, identified by numbers like 7 × 35 or 10 × 50. The first number, the magnification, tells you how many times wider something looks through the binoculars than it does without them. The second is the width of the light-collecting lens in millimeters. The larger the lens, the more light it can collect. You might think that larger magnification and lenses are always better, but that isn't true. The bigger they are, the heavier the binoculars get. Different types of binoculars are made for different uses.

The Microscope

The microscope is a close relative to the telescope, but we know even less about its origins. Like the telescope, it was probably an accidental discovery by a Dutch spectacle-maker. The first microscopes were made around 1590, but it is not clear who really invented the microscope. Two brothers, Hans and Zacharias Jansen, who like Hans Lippershey lived in Middelburg, often get the credit, but they were never able to prove their claim. Zacharias Jansen was even suspected of fraud!

A simple positive lens can magnify small objects; it's what we call a magnifying glass. As we saw earlier, it bends light rays so they seem to come from a larger object. By putting two positive lenses together in the right way, you can make a microscope, which enlarges objects even more than a simple magnifier.

In a simple microscope the farther lens projects an enlarged real image that you see through the one closer to your eye, the eyepiece. In practical microscopes, assemblies of two or more lenses replace the single lenses shown.

As you can see when you look closely, a microscope is not dramatically different from a telescope. It was no coincidence that they were invented at about the same time in the same place. In fact, telescope optics can work as microscope optics when adjusted properly, although they don't work very well. Galileo could view close objects with telescope lenses, but he had to use a tube two or three times longer than in his telescope.

Like the world of the very distant, the world of the very small has its mysteries. Without the microscope, we would know little or nothing about germs, living cells, or the appearance of insects.

Perhaps the most fascinating microscopic discoveries were made by a Dutch cloth merchant who lived in the town of Delft, Antony van Leeuwenhoek. He used only simple magnifying lenses but powerful ones polished with an exacting precision that magnified more than some modern microscopes. He may have gotten his start looking through a lens at cloth to see previously invisible details. His fame came after he looked at a drop of cloudy green water from a marshy lake and found it full of tiny plants and animals. He knew they were alive because they moved and changed, and he wrote about them to the Royal Society of London. Today, we know that van Leeuwenhoek was the first man to see the world of microscopic plants and animals.

Modern Optical Instruments

A couple of lenses in a tube made a marvelous optical instrument in the seventeenth century. Craftsmen put the simple lenses into housings that today look like works of art. However, the optics of those early instruments were not very good by today's standards. The simple lenses used in those instruments had serious limitations. They focused different colors to different points, forming a blur of colors around white objects. Often they showed only the center of a scene clearly, with the edges blurred.

As people learned more about optics, they found out how to fix those problems. They made microscopes and telescopes work better by replacing single lenses with achromatic lenses, or with pairs of lenses. They found that special coatings could reduce stray light. They learned how to make better lenses and how to use computers to design complex optical systems. In modern instruments several lenses may serve the same purpose as one lens in a seventeenth-century instrument.

The first microscopes and telescopes were made for human eyes to see visible light. Today, human eyes rarely look through many sophisticated optical instruments. Giant telescopes direct light not to an astronomer's eye but to a sensitive photographic plate or electronic detector that collects light for hours. No person will look through the Hubble space telescope, but many astronomers will study the images it records, searching for details that their eyes could never have seen through the telescope.

Many modern telescopes and microscopes do not use visible light. Astronomers look at the universe in most of the electromagnetic spectrum. They have special telescopes to look for radio waves, microwaves, infrared, ultraviolet light, X rays, and gamma rays. Some microscopes don't use any sort of electromagnetic radiation. The electron microscope can see details invisible in light by using electrons, tiny fragments of atoms with negative electric charge.

Making Pictures:
Cameras and Television

The great Dutch painter Rembrandt was born in 1609, not long after Dutch spectacle-makers had started making microscopes and telescopes. For more than two centuries afterward, making pictures was the work of artists. Telescopes and microscopes could help the eye see better, but they could not make pictures to hang on the wall. If a rich merchant wanted a portrait of himself, he hired an artist to paint it. If optics entered the picture at all, it was only as part of the portrait. The merchant might be wearing eyeglasses or holding a telescope, but the only optics the artist used were his eyes.

We have seen already how positive lenses can make real images that can be projected on paper or a wall. Early scientists knew this, too. But just projecting an image is not enough to make a picture. Move the lens, and the image goes away. People couldn't take pictures with optics until they learned how to save images. That knowledge came with the birth of photography in the nineteenth century.

The photographic camera was the first optical device to take pictures. Others have followed. Movie cameras followed still cameras. Now we have television cameras so small and inexpensive that some families have them in their homes. We also have projectors, devices that put pictures onto screens, and holograms, which can project three-dimensional images. Their workings depend not just on lenses but on the photographic films and electronic detectors we discussed earlier. We'll look at these imaging optics in a rough order of complexity, starting with the simple camera and moving on to television and three-dimensional holography.

Simple Cameras

Photography as we know it is 150 years old. It was born in 1839, when Frenchman Louis Daguerre invented the first process to record pictures. British scientist Sir John Herschel coined the word *photography* in early 1839, but pictures made with Daguerre's process were called "daguerreotypes."

Even before Daguerre's time, people knew that light would convert some light-colored silver compounds to black metallic silver. That looked like a good way to record the pattern of bright and dark areas in an image formed by a lens. The problem was in freezing that picture, so more light didn't break down the rest of the silver compound and turn the whole scene black. Daguerre found a way to stop the process. He shut off the light and added mercury to form a stable white compound with metallic silver. Then he removed the silver compound that broke down in light, so more light could not form more silver metal.

Daguerre's process was not like today's standard photographic films in one important way. It didn't use negatives. Like a slide, the exposed daguerreotype plate became the finished picture.

That may sound simple, but daguerreotypes were hard to make. Soon pioneering photographers found how to coat glass plates and films with a new silver compound. They also found out how to make negatives. The negative is an extra step, but it let them make many copies of a single picture.

Photographic films have come a long way since then. If you wanted to have your photograph taken in the mid-1800s, you would have to sit perfectly still in bright sunlight for a minute or two for a black-and-white picture. That was an improvement over six to ten minutes for Daguerre's first photographs, but it still wasn't easy. Now we have cameras and films that can take a black-and-white photo in bright sunlight in a few thousandths of a second. We also have color films. Now there are so many different types of film that you must be careful to pick the right one in order to get the type of pictures you want.

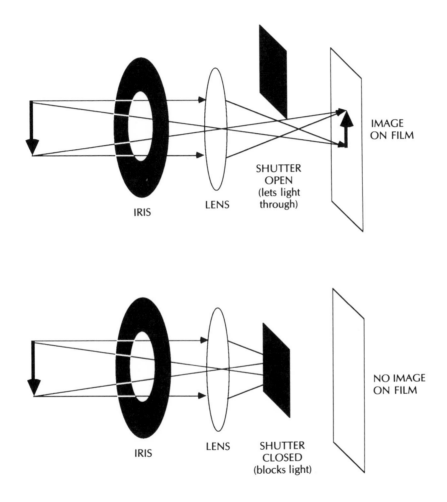

FIGURE 9-1 *A camera includes a shutter, which keeps light from reaching the film unless you are taking a picture, and an iris, which opens and closes to control how much light reaches the film when the shutter is open. Together the shutter speed and iris opening control exposure of the film.*

HOW CAMERAS WORK

So far, we have made camera optics sound very simple. You might think all you need is to take a lens and focus a real image onto a piece of film. However, even a simple camera needs more than that. You must be able to control light getting into the camera. That's the job of a shutter, which normally keeps light out of the camera, except when you click it. Then it lets light through for a fraction of a second—long enough to expose the film—before shutting again. You also need a way to adjust how much light gets in while the shutter is open. That's the job of the iris. Like the iris of your eye, it opens and closes. The wider it is open, the more light gets in. Photographers adjust iris opening and shutter speed so pictures do not come out too light or too dark. We show those components in Figure 9–1.

A single positive lens might suffice for a cheap toy camera but not for a good one. As in a telescope, a simple lens does not focus all light going through it to the same point. Optical engineers solve this problem

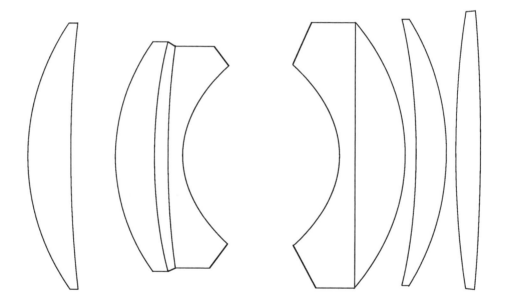

FIGURE 9–2 *Side view of a camera lens assembly, showing the components used to make sure all light is focused exactly on the film.*

by putting together two or more lenses in an assembly such as the one in Figure 9–2.

A good camera also must be able to take pictures of objects that are different distances from it. The camera must focus light exactly on the film to make a clear picture. Remember, however, that how far the image is from the lens depends on how far the object is from the lens, as shown in Figure 9–3. The nearer the object is to the lens, the farther away the image is. If you want to focus the image precisely on the film, you must move the lens or the film.

Simple, inexpensive cameras can get away with not doing either, as

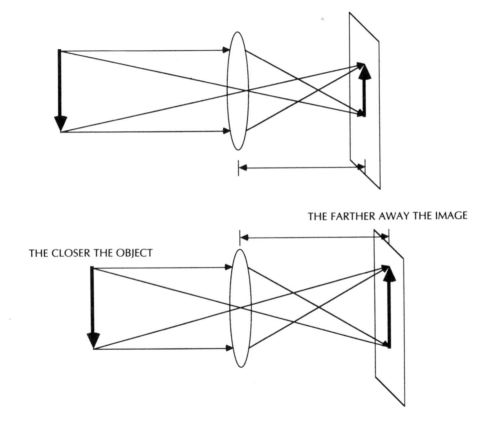

THE FARTHER AWAY THE IMAGE

THE CLOSER THE OBJECT

FIGURE 9–3 *The closer an object is to the lens, the farther away is its image. Thus the position of the lens and film must be adjusted if the object moves closer, as at bottom.*

long as they don't try to take close-ups. The focal distances don't change much when objects are far from the lens. Suppose you're using a camera lens with three-centimeter (1.2 inch) focal length. It forms a real image of an object three meters (ten feet) away, 2.97 centimeters behind the lens. Move the object closer, to two meters away, and the image barely moves to 2.96 centimeters from the lens. That's still in focus. However, something just ten centimeters (four inches) away would be imaged at 2.31 centimeters from the lens, clearly out of focus.

Good cameras have lenses that move to focus precisely on objects at different distances. If you have such a camera, look at how the lens adjusts. Changing the focus from ten feet (three meters) to infinity (distant objects) moves the lens just a little. Changing the focus from three to four feet moves the lens much more. Many photographers adjust the focus by hand, looking through the lens and watching the image. Some new cameras can do it automatically, by measuring the distance to an object with a short pulse of sound waves at frequencies too high for you to hear.

PINHOLE CAMERAS

You don't have to have a lens to make a camera. You can use the pinhole lens we described in Chapter 3. Only a few light rays can pass through the tiny pinhole, but those that do spread out at exactly the angle they entered, forming a real image.

You can take photographs with a pinhole camera, although so little light gets through the pinhole that it takes a few minutes to expose the film, making it not very useful. However, a pinhole camera is a practical way to look at the sun, especially during a partial eclipse. Make a very small hole in the front of a shoebox and aim the box at the sun (don't look directly at the sun yourself). Keep the back of the box in the shade. Line the box up properly with the sun, and you should see an image of the sun projected on the inside of the shoebox.

Movie Cameras

A movie camera (but *not* a television camera) works much like an ordinary still camera. The two cameras use similar films. Both have lenses that are adjusted to focus light sharply onto the film. However, the movie camera adds something else—motion.

The only thing moving in a moving picture is the film. Movie film is made of many still photos, taken a fraction of a second apart. When you see a movie, each photo appears on the screen for a tiny fraction of a second. Your eyes and your brain blend them together, and you see what looks like motion.

How does it work? The part of the camera that moves the film has small teeth that fit into holes on the edges of the film. The teeth grab the film and move it into position. Then they hold the film still while the shutter opens to expose one "frame" of the film. After the shutter closes, the teeth move the film along so the exposed part is out of the light, and a fresh frame will be exposed. Standard professional movie cameras expose twenty-four frames each second. Most home movie cameras expose sixteen frames per second.

If you look at movie film, you can see that each frame looks like a small, still picture. Look carefully, and you can see that the people move slightly between frames. When the film is projected on the screen, the frames come so fast that the pictures blend together and seem to move. (Sometimes you can see interesting effects by blinking your eyes during a movie, because it can break the illusion of motion.)

Projectors

A camera lens projects an image onto film close to the lens, so the image is much smaller than the object. A projector works in the opposite way, projecting a large image of a small object (a piece of transparent film—a slide or movie frame). The simplest type of projector is a positive lens held close to the film. It works in the same way that the lens in our example in Chapter 3 projected a big image of a light-bulb label on the ceiling.

Real slide and movie projectors are more complex. An ordinary slide projector includes a lamp (to shine light through the slide), a lens to focus the lamp light onto the slide, and a lens to focus the light passing through the slide onto the screen, as shown in Figure 9–4. Like the lens

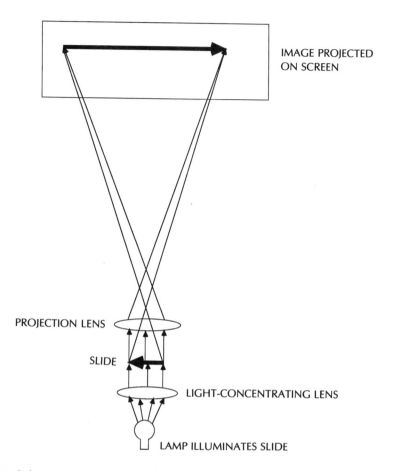

IMAGE PROJECTED ON SCREEN

PROJECTION LENS

SLIDE

LIGHT-CONCENTRATING LENS

LAMP ILLUMINATES SLIDE

FIGURE 9–4 *A slide or movie projector shines light from a bright bulb through film, forming an enlarged image of the film on a screen. Screens are used because they reflect light efficiently, but you also can project slides on a white wall.*

on a camera, a slide projector lens can be moved back and forth to focus the image sharply. The bulb must be bright, the screen reflective, and the room dark to show an image that many people can see.

Movie projectors work almost the same way, but they project a series of still pictures on the screen. As in a movie camera, the film steps through the projector, staying still long enough for a shutter to let light through and flash the image onto the screen. If the shutter and film movement are not adjusted correctly, the images flutter or show the bar between frames.

You see things happen faster or slower than normal by showing movies at a speed different from the one at which they were taken. In slow-motion photography, frames are shown slower than they were taken. You might take ninety-six frames a second, then show twenty-four frames per second to slow action to a quarter of normal speed. Time-lapse photography works the other way, taking pictures more slowly than they are shown. If you want to watch the grass grow, you could take one movie frame every ten minutes and project the frames at normal speed; in ten seconds, you could see a day's worth of growth; in a little over a minute, you could watch a week's worth.

Television Cameras

The optics of a television camera are much like those of a movie camera. The big difference is in how the pictures are taken. The television camera focuses light onto a sensor that turns the pattern of light into an electronic signal. We described television image sensors in Chapter 6.

Photographic film takes a picture all at once. A television camera doesn't. It electronically scans over the image, the way your eyes scan over the page to read these words. The electronic signal from the camera records the pattern it scans in a sequence, the way your brain reads these words in series as it scans the page. Look carefully at a television screen, and you can see the pattern of lines scanned by the camera and shown in the screen.

Television cameras scan in a standard way, so their signals can be seen on all television sets. In the United States, Canada, Mexico, Japan, and some other countries, you remember, the standard is scanning 525 lines on a screen thirty times a second. Now engineers want to improve the looks of television pictures by using a new format with over 1000 lines per screen.

Television Screens

A television picture tube takes the electronic signal generated by a television camera and transmitted by a television station and turns it back into a picture. Almost all television sets use what are called "cathode ray tubes," or CRTs, which also are used in computer displays. The CRT fires a beam of electrons at the screen you see. The strength of the beam depends on the strength of the signal. The tube steers the beam so it scans lines across the screen, as shown in Figure 9–5.

The inside of the CRT is coated with a phosphor, which glows when electrons hit it. It keeps on glowing for a fraction of a second after the electron beam passes over it. By the time the phosphor grows dim, the electron beam is ready to scan over it and make it glow again. As long as the tube works right, the eye sees a steady picture that does not flicker.

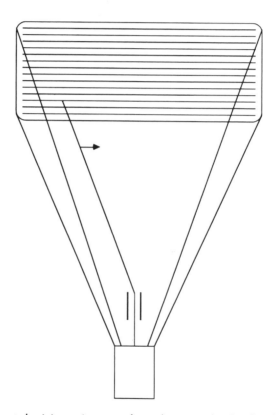

FIGURE 9–5 *In a television picture tube, plates at the back of the tube scan a beam of electrons across the screen. The strength of the beam is controlled by the video signal. A phosphor on the screen glows when electrons hit it. The stronger the electron beam, the brighter the glow and the picture.*

Like a movie, a television set gives the illusion of motion. At any instant, the picture on your screen is fixed. Yet it also changes steadily as the electron beam paints a new picture on the screen. That new picture is a little different from the last, just as each movie frame is different from the one before it. To make sure that change isn't visible to your eye, the CRT paints every other line. First it paints 1, 3, 5, 7, 9, etc., then—after finishing the odd lines—it paints the even ones. Although we say television shows thirty frames a second, it really shows sixty half-frames a second.

Television sets with very large or small screens may not use cathode ray tubes. Most screens larger than about twenty-five inches (the diagonal width of the screen, not the width straight across) project pictures formed on smaller screens. Tiny television screens sometimes use liquid-crystal displays like those on digital watches, rather than ordinary picture tubes. The liquid crystals cannot show as many lines as a picture tube (yet), but they require much less power and are much smaller.

As with photography, black-and-white television came before color and is much easier to explain. Color television pictures are made of three colors, red, blue, and green. The red, green, and blue colored images are put together so we see a full-color picture.

To take color television pictures, you need a special camera with three different sensors, one for each color. Optics inside the camera separate the three colors and send each one to the right sensor. Each color sensor then makes its own electrical signal, and the three are combined into a single television signal.

At the picture tube the three color signals are separated. Color picture tubes contain three electron guns, one for each color. The screen has separate sets of phosphor cells for each color. If you look very closely, you sometimes can see the array of tiny red, green, and blue dots on the screen. The red gun aims electrons only at cells that emit red light; the green gun at the green phosphor, and the blue gun at the blue phosphor. Getting it right isn't easy, and if your set is not working right, you can see some strange colors.

Other Displays

Television screens, photographs, slides, and motion pictures all are examples of displays that show us images. There are many other types of displays, and we can only talk about a few here.

Most computer screens and video displays use the same CRT technology as television screens but often not the same standards. For example, the number of lines may be different from those shown on a standard television screen. You can see the differences if you compare the screens on different computers to each other or to a television set.

Calculators, digital watches, some portable computers, and an increasing number of other displays use liquid crystal displays. A liquid crystal, sandwiched between glass or plastic plates, reflects light differently when electricity is applied to it. Normally, the crystal reflects light well, but electricity can make it absorb light. The electricity forms a pattern of electric charge that makes the dark numbers you see on a pocket calculator display. Liquid crystals don't make light like a CRT or light bulb, so they need very little electrical power. That makes them good choices for digital watches or light-powered calculators. They also show channel selections on television sets and display cooking time on microwave ovens. However, because liquid crystals don't make light, you can't see them in the dark. For displays you must see in the dark—like a clock radio—you are better off with the LED displays described in Chapter 5.

Holography

All the displays we have described so far are flat, or two-dimensional. However, a technique called "holography" can make three-dimensional displays. The concept was invented in 1948 by Dennis Gabor, and it earned him the 1972 Nobel Prize in Physics. Few people paid much attention to it, however, until Emmett Leith and Juris Upatnieks made the first three-dimensional hologram using a laser in the early 1960s.

Holography relies on complex interactions among light waves. A hologram itself is a flat pattern recorded on film or a sheet of glass or plastic when two beams of light come together, as shown in Figure 9–6.

Both come from the same light source, but one has been reflected from the object and one hasn't. Lasers usually are used to make holograms because the light must be coherent, with the waves in the two beams in phase with each other.

When the hologram is later illuminated by a light similar to the original source, from the same direction, it scatters light to "reconstruct" a

MAKING A HOLOGRAM

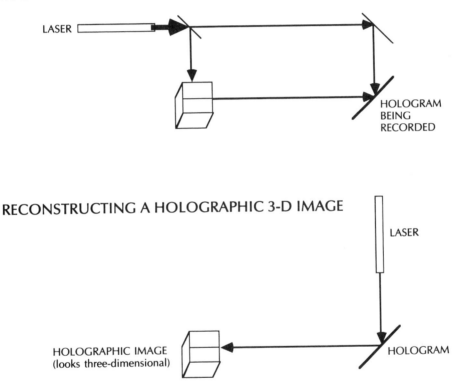

LASER

HOLOGRAM
BEING
RECORDED

RECONSTRUCTING A HOLOGRAPHIC 3-D IMAGE

LASER

HOLOGRAPHIC IMAGE
(looks three-dimensional)

HOLOGRAM

FIGURE 9–6 *The making of a hologram is shown at top. The beam from a laser is split in two. Half lights up a three-dimensional box; the other goes a different path to a photographic plate. Light from the box is combined with the other beam to make the hologram. After the hologram is developed, you can see an image of the original box by shining light at the hologram in the same direction in which the second beam originally hit it. This picture shows a laser making the image, but you don't need a laser to see most holograms.*

three-dimensional image of the original object, as shown at the bottom of Figure 9–6. The details are too complex to describe here, but the result is striking. The photograph in Figure 9–7 is not of a real pair of eyeglasses, but of "holographic spectacles," an image by British artist Michael Wenyon. If you look closely at a real hologram, you will see that it looks grainy, as a beach looks grainy when you look at it closely. The colors also are not lifelike. Otherwise, holographic images look real enough to touch.

Although lasers are needed to make holograms, you don't have to have a laser to see them. Many can be viewed in ordinary "white" light. If you look at these holograms from different angles, you will see different colors. That's how they earned the name of "rainbow" holograms.

Engineers now can mass-produce holograms by pressing patterns

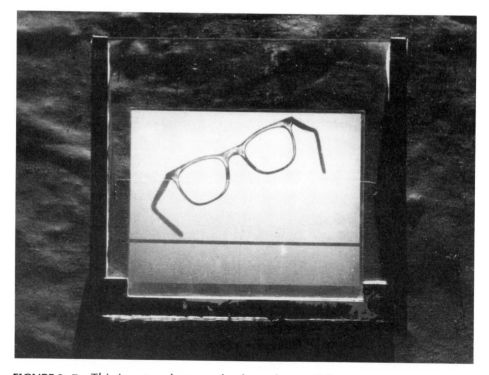

FIGURE 9–7   *This is not a photograph of eyeglasses. What you see is a picture of a hologram, "Holographic Spectacles," by British artist Michael Wenyon. (Courtesy of Michael Wenyon)*

into shiny plastic-coated foil. You can see these "embossed" holograms in many places, such as on the covers of paperback books, on stickers, and even on credit cards. If you look at them from just the right angle, they can give you an idea what holograms look like. However, the best holograms look so much better that you want to reach out and touch them.

Guiding Light:
Fiber Optics and
Optical Communications

All the optics we have talked about so far depend on light going in straight lines. However, sometimes you may not want light to follow a straight path. Is there any way to make light follow a curved path or to build pipes that would take light anywhere we want it to go? Light won't really fit into pipes, but optical fibers will do almost the same job.

Fiber optics is a new branch of optics, but it has been the fastest growing in recent years. The first usable optical fibers were made in the 1950s to carry light and images to and from hard-to-reach places. In the late 1960s, engineers realized that fiber optics might carry telephone calls better than wires. A series of spectacular successes followed. Today fiber-optic cables carry telephone calls across the United States. In 1988, the first transatlantic fiber-optic cable will begin carrying phone calls between North America and Europe. Let's see how fiber optics came so far so fast.

Light Piping

Sometimes people think of ideas long before they know how to make the ideas work. In 1880, a young engineer from Concord, Massachusetts, applied for a patent on a new way to light buildings. William Wheeler had just returned to his home town after four years in Japan, where he helped start that country's first engineering college. He must have known about the electric light bulb that Thomas Edison and Joseph Swan had invented a few years earlier, but he thought he had a better idea. He

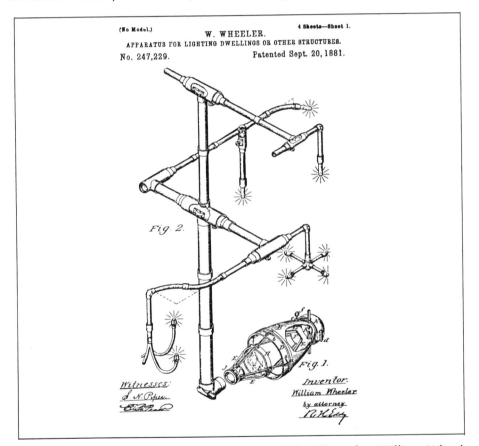

FIGURE 10–1 *The plan for piping light through buildings that William Wheeler patented in 1881. (Reproduced with permission of the publisher, Howard W. Sams & Co., Indianapolis, Indiana, from* Understanding Fiber Optics, *Jeff Hecht, copyright © 1987)*

wanted to equip each house with a central electric arc lamp and to pipe light from that bright lamp to other rooms. He patented a way to make pipes with inside mirror surfaces to carry light between rooms, as shown in Figure 10–1 from his patent.

Another of Wheeler's optical ideas, the Wheeler reflector, was for many years used on streetlamps. However, Edison's light bulb was much more practical than Wheeler's plan for arc lamps and light pipes. Mirror surfaces do not reflect 100 percent of the incident light; a little is always absorbed. Because light would be reflected many times in the pipe, the absorption would add up quickly, and little light would get through the pipe. Dirty light pipes would have been a housecleaning nightmare.

Total Internal Reflection

The key concept behind the optical fiber actually dates back long before Wheeler, to a discovery by early experimenters in optics. Sometimes light couldn't get out of glass because of a phenomenon called total internal reflection.

Earlier we saw how light is refracted as it passes from one transparent material into another. When light goes from air into glass or any material with a higher refractive index, the light rays are straightened out, as we saw in Figure 2–5. Suppose, however, that the light ray is going in the other direction, into a material with a lower refractive index, such as from glass into air. Then the light emerges at a steeper angle.

What happens if light in the glass hits the border with air at a steep angle? The light ray going into the air must leave at an even steeper angle, as shown in Figure 10–2. At what is called the "critical angle," the light would try to emerge at a right angle to the normal, or right along the surface. Tilt the light in the glass beyond this "critical angle" and it can't get out. This is called total internal reflection, because all the light is reflected back into the glass.

You can see total internal reflection in a right-angle prism, with two forty-five-degree angles and one ninety-degree angle. Hold the prism with one of the narrower sides flat toward your face and the other pointing up. You might expect to see straight through, but total internal reflection shows you the ceiling. Such prisms are used in binoculars,

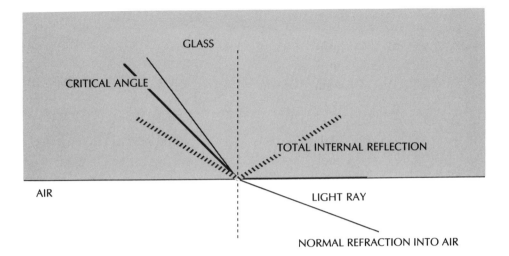

FIGURE 10–2 *Light going from glass into air normally is bent at a steeper angle than that at which it was traveling in the glass. If the light hits the surface at a glancing angle, it is all reflected back into the glass; this is called "total internal reflection."*

periscopes, and some other optical instruments. Total internal reflection is not limited to prisms, however. It also can guide light in a glass rod—which is where fiber optics comes along.

Light Guiding

Suppose light going through a piece of glass with two flat, parallel surfaces hits one side at a glancing angle. Total internal reflection bounces it back into the glass. When it hits the other side, it will strike at the same glancing angle—and total internal reflection will again keep it in the glass. That means the light will keep on bouncing down the glass. The same is true if the glass is a straight cylindrical rod.

In fact, the rod does not have to be straight. If it is bent at a small angle, light inside it will hit the opposite surfaces at nearly the same angle and be reflected around the bend, as shown in Figure 10–3.

Ancient glassblowers may have noticed such light guiding, but they kept it a secret of their trade. Physicists were well aware of it in the nineteenth century. Starting in the 1850s, noted Irish-born physicist John

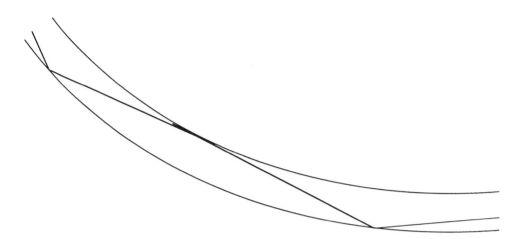

FIGURE 10–3 *Total internal reflection can bend light around corners in a curved glass rod.*

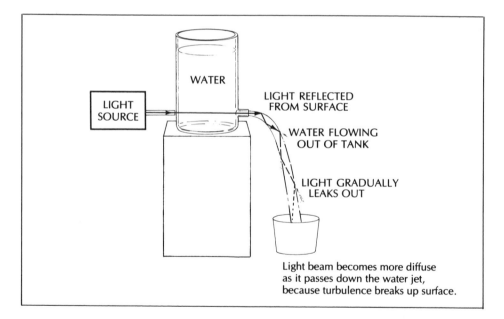

FIGURE 10–4 *In a series of lectures, John Tyndall demonstrated total internal reflection by letting light shine down a stream of water coming from a barrel. (Reproduced with permission of the publisher, Howard W. Sams & Co., Indianapolis, Indiana, from* Understanding Fiber Optics, *Jeff Hecht, copyright ©* 1987)

Tyndall showed light-guiding in lectures in Europe and North America. He shined light along a stream of water flowing out of a barrel, as shown in Figure 10–4. The light was reflected along the flowing water, gradually fading as it leaked out the sides of the stream.

Unfortunately, this simple light guide does not work very well. Light leaks out if the glass touches other things, even if they're not transparent. The glass of Tyndall's time wasn't very clear anyway, so it couldn't have carried light far. People thought Tyndall's demonstration was an interesting trick, but little more.

Practical Optical Fibers

No practical solution to the light-guiding problem came until the early 1950s, but it proved surprisingly simple. Brian O'Brien, Sr., working at the American Optical Company in Southbridge, Massachusetts, surrounded the glass rod with a layer of glass with a lower refractive index. Light in the core bounced back if it hit the outer "cladding" layer at a glancing angle. The cladding kept the core from touching anything else, so light could not leak out. At about the same time, Harry Hopkins and Narinder Kapany were working on the same idea in England.

O'Brien, Hopkins, and Kapany all were working with glass rods so thin they were really fibers. Fibers of glass date back a century. In 1887, British physicist Charles Vernon Boys made the first thin glass fibers by firing an arrow attached to molten glass. However, Boys and others who followed him apparently never thought of shining light down the fibers.

Glass optical fibers are strong, flexible, and do not break easily. Most single fibers are 0.125 millimeter in diameter, but normally they are coated with plastic that makes them 0.25 to 0.5 millimeter thick. With that plastic coating, they are a little thicker and stiffer than the bristles on a toothbrush. The core usually is only about 0.01 millimeter across, but some types of fibers do have larger cores.

Optical fibers also can be made of transparent plastics. Plastics are not as clear as the best glasses, but they are more flexible and even less likely to break. Plastic fibers usually are larger and thicker than glass fibers, and some are a couple of millimeters across.

Fiber-Optic Imaging

O'Brien wanted to send images from one place to another. You can't do that with a single glass rod or fiber. The light it carries is mixed together at the end. If you looked through a single fiber at a spot that was half white and half black, you would see only gray.

To send an image, you need a bundle of fibers. Each fiber carries part of the image, so when you look through the bundle you see a set of spots, as in Figure 10–5. The example shows only a few fibers and a few spots, but most bundles have many more fibers, and the spots are so small that you don't notice them, like the dots that make up a television picture.

For a fiber bundle to carry an image, each fiber must be in the same place at each end. You wouldn't see the A in Figure 10–5 if the fibers

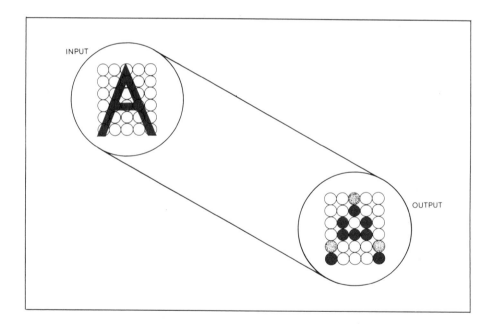

FIGURE 10–5 *A bundle of fibers collects light from one end and carries it to the other. As long as all the fibers are in the same places at both ends, the bundle can carry an image. (Reproduced with permission of the publisher, Howard W. Sams & Co., Indianapolis, Indiana, from* Understanding Fiber Optics, *Jeff Hecht, copyright © 1987)*

were scrambled on each end. Sometimes fiber bundles are scrambled on purpose, because they don't have to carry images—just carry light to a hard-to-reach spot. Fiber bundles also can light up patterns. One end of the bundle could collect light from a bulb, while the other end spelled out the word WALK on a traffic signal.

Other types of optics can do many of the same jobs as bundled optical fibers. Why bother with fiber bundles? The main reason is to get light to and from places it could not otherwise reach.

A dramatic example is looking inside the human body. A doctor can insert a fiber-optic bundle called an "endoscope" down a patient's throat to see into the stomach. Some fibers carry light to illuminate the stomach. Others collect light that the stomach reflects, so the doctor can see inside to check for disease. Endoscopes can let doctors see inside other parts of the body that they couldn't examine otherwise without cutting into the patient. Endoscopes also can deliver laser energy to treat some diseases, such as cancer or bleeding ulcers.

Fiber-Optic Communications

The biggest use of optical fibers is to carry messages. Engineers call that "communications," or sometimes "telecommunications." You communicate when you talk or send letters. You communicate over the telephone, and people communicate to you by television. People communicate by wires, satellites, and radio waves. They also communicate by light.

Now we communicate through optical fibers, but long ago people sent signals through the air by light. An Indian scout on a hilltop might see a herd of buffalo far away and want to tell the rest of the tribe a few miles away on the plains. He could do that by lighting a fire, which the rest of the tribe would know meant that the buffalo were coming. He was communicating by light.

Today, fiber-optic, or light-wave, communication is part of the long-distance telephone system. Wires connect the phone in your home to switching computers, which connect to fiber-optic cables. The telephone converts your voice to electricity. Then, a laser or LED changes the electricity into pulses of light that go through an optical fiber. At the other end of the fiber, a detector turns the light back into electric currents. The currents go through wires to a telephone that converts them into sound heard by the person you are talking with.

There is a big difference between those two signals. The fire on the hill said only one thing—that the buffalo were coming. Your voice on the fiber-optic telephone line can say many things. In fact, the same optical fiber probably carries hundreds or thousands of other conversations.

We can count the difference, by comparing the number of bits being sent. A *bit* is a unit of information, a "yes" or "no," or a one or zero. The signal fire carried only one bit—news that the buffalo were coming. No fire meant no buffalo. That simple code could work because the tribe knew beforehand that a fire meant the buffalo were coming. Fiber-optic communication systems can carry hundreds of millions of bits each second. Before long, new systems will carry billions of bits.

Early Optical Communications

Optical communication did not stop with smoke signals. The first communication system faster than messengers on horseback was the optical telegraph. Claude Chappe built it in the 1790s in France, when the country was in turmoil.

The optical telegraph was a series of towers on tall hills, with movable arms attached. A man with a telescope sat in each tower. Movement of the arms spelled out a code, which the operator could read through his telescope, then relay to the next tower by moving the arms on his tower.

In a matter of minutes, the optical telegraph could send messages hundreds of miles, a distance it would have taken days to travel before. France built more optical telegraphs, and other countries built them, too. However, the optical telegraph was far from perfect. Even in those days, it was expensive to pay a man to sit at each station. The operator had to see the next tower, so the optical telegraph shut down at night and in bad weather. Smoke from the city of London often blocked one English optical telegraph.

Wires replaced the hilltop towers when the electric telegraph was perfected in the mid-1800s, but the optical telegraph was not forgotten.

Its memory lives on in the names of countless "Telegraph Hills" around the world. Well into this century, railroads used movable arms, called "semaphores," to tell train engineers if it was safe to go ahead. (You often find semaphores beside the tracks of model trains.)

The telephone came after the electric telegraph, but optical communication was not forgotten. In 1880, four years after he made the first working telephone, Alexander Graham Bell showed that light, as well as wires, could carry voices.

Bell was not satisfied with sending voices through wires as electric currents. He wanted to send them through the air as beams of light. On a trip to England, he saw an early light detector, which changed the way it carried electric current when light struck it. He took that idea back to his laboratory in Washington, D.C., and he and his assistant Sumner Tainter made sound control a beam of light. They made their light detector drive a little speaker. In February 1880 Bell wrote his father, "I have heard a ray of the sun laugh and cough and sing!"

The delighted Bell thought of naming his newborn daughter Photophone after his invention. Luckily for the girl, common sense prevailed. Unluckily for Bell, the photophone never proved practical. Wires are easy to run from place to place, but beams of light want to go in straight lines. Clouds, fog, and rain can get in their way. A photophone might let you talk to someone next door, but how could you send beams of light around corners, or from one city to the next? No engineers knew the answers a century ago, so they preferred the telephone. Bell and Tainter moved on to sound recording and gave the original photophone to the Smithsonian Institution, where it lay nearly forgotten for almost a century.

The Start of Fiber-Optic Communications

The birth of the laser in 1960 revived interest in optical communications. Scientists knew that beams of light could carry huge amounts of information, much more than radio waves or microwaves. The growth of communications meant that more and more information had to be sent places. Television had come on the scene. Telephones had become common. By 1960, more than a hundred billion calls were being made each year in the United States, and the country had 74 million telephones.

The telephone industry's big problem was not the wires going to homes. Those wires carry only one phone call at a time to a phone company in your town. The problem was in lines going between towns, which carry many calls at once. As more people called more often, those long-distance lines were running out of room.

The first scientists to study laser optical communications tried to send the beam through the air, or even through pipes. The first people to suggest using fiber optics were Charles K. Kao and George Hockham, who in 1966 worked at Standard Telecommunication Laboratories in Britain. They said that if glass could be purified enough, optical fibers could carry many phone calls at once over longer distances than wires.

Their idea excited many people, but it was only an idea. Kao and Hockham thought optical fibers could be made clear enough so that 10 percent of the light would remain after passing through 500 meters (1640 feet) of fiber. However, optical fibers available then could not send light that far. Only 10 percent remained after passing through just 10 meters (33 feet) of fiber.

What was needed was clearer glass. Four years later, Robert Maurer, Donald Keck, and Peter Schultz made the first real "low-loss" fibers at the Corning Glass Works. Since then, scientists have made glass purer and clearer than Kao and Hockham thought possible. In the best fibers available today, over 10 percent of the light remains after traveling 50 kilometers (31 miles).

Telephone companies around the world now use fiber optics to carry calls between cities. Long-distance companies such as the American Telephone & Telegraph Corporation and MCI Telecommunications have fiber-optic networks that run from the Atlantic to the Pacific oceans. Regional telephone companies run fiber-optic cables between cities and towns. In the next few years, undersea fiber-optic cables will begin carrying telephone conversations through the depths of both the Atlantic and Pacific oceans, making international phone calls clearer than ever before.

The Fibered World

You may not think it very exciting to run fiber-optic cables between towns. Your calls may get cheaper and cheaper, but it's not easy to tell the difference. The real excitement in fiber optics has yet to come—bringing optical fibers to homes.

A fiber-optic connection to your house could bring more than clearer phone calls. It could carry television programs and computer data as well. It might automatically send meter readings to the gas and electric companies. It will bring lots of new possibilities, and we'll talk a little more about some of them in the last chapter.

11

Light and Life

Life needs light. Put a green plant in a dark closet, and it will die, starved of the light energy it needs to grow. Animals can live in the dark, but they can't make their own food. Most dark-dwellers eat things that once grew in the light. If you look very, very hard you can find a few exceptions, strange creatures that dwell in the ocean depths and get their energy from heat leaking from the earth's core. But all the world's people, and all the plants and animals that we know, would soon die without the energy that sunlight brings.

Our daily lives depend on light energy. Light also can help heal. Lasers can reach inside the eye to help cure blindness. Lasers also can perform bloodless surgery and other medical miracles, as we'll learn later in this chapter.

Solar Energy in Nature

On a clear day, when the sun is due overhead, sunlight delivers 1.35 kilowatts (1350 watts) of power to a square meter of the earth's surface. That's as much power as a small portable electric heater, but you don't have to pay the electric bill when sunlight does the heating. If the sun is lower, less sunlight reaches the ground, but it still keeps us warm. The ground, water, and air all absorb the sun's energy and release enough at night to keep temperatures from getting too cold.

You can see how sunlight warms the earth in many ways. In winter the sun is low and the weather is cold. In summer, both the sun and the temperatures are higher. Temperatures are warmer near the equator than at the poles for the same reason—the sun never rises high at the poles but is nearly overhead in the tropics.

Using Solar Energy

Plants and animals use the sun's energy in many ways. Green plants collect the sun's energy by "photosynthesis." The word means using light (*photo*) to make (*synthesize*) sugars and starches, which are the plant's way of storing energy. Thus plants make food for themselves, for the animals that eat them, and ultimately for people. Some animals use the sun's energy in other ways, usually to warm them, like a lizard warms itself in the sun.

People use the sun's energy in other ways than for food. Solar cells can turn light energy into electricity, but not very efficiently. It would take 0.44 square meter (a square about two feet on a side) to make enough electric power to light a 60-watt bulb. "Solar-powered" calculators work, even under much dimmer light, because they don't take much power.

We can also use the sun's energy to make something hot. Some homes use the sun to heat water. If your house has many windows facing south, sunlight helps warm it.

Except for electricity from nuclear power plants, most energy we use originally came from the sun. Wood was grown by sunlight. Coal, oil, and gas are fossilized remains of ancient plants. Water power gets its energy from rain that falls after the sun evaporates water from lakes and oceans. Even the winds are powered by the sun.

Light and Medicine

Light can help diagnose illness. When someone says you look "peaked," "pale," or "flushed," they are looking at the color of your skin to see how well you are. If you are bruised, your skin changes color at the point of injury. If your throat is sore, it probably looks red and inflamed.

Those color changes often show how blood flows in your body. Extra blood is sent to areas that are hurt or infected. Swelling also is part of the way your body deals with illness. The color changes are not intended to show where a problem is, but doctors—and many other people—have learned how to interpret them.

The eye of a skilled physician is a good tool for identifying some diseases. To find other problems a physician or a medical technician may look at cells under a microscope. Certain changes in the cell may indicate if it has become cancerous. Changes in the way blood cells look might indicate other problems.

Light also is a vital tool in testing the eye. Light lets an eye doctor look inside your eye to see if your retina is healthy. Special optical instruments can measure how well the eye focuses light.

Our bodies use light in other ways. One is to make vitamin D, which we need to form healthy bones and teeth. Most foods do not contain vitamin D, but we can make it from a related chemical common in food. Our bodies bring that chemical to our skin, where sunlight converts it into vitamin D. Adults normally get enough sunlight to make all the vitamin D they need, but children may not because they are growing faster and need more of the vitamin, so vitamin D is added to milk.

The color of your skin affects how much vitamin D you can make. The darker your skin, the less sunlight can penetrate, and the less vitamin D your skin can make. That's why dark-skinned people are more likely to need vitamin D than light-skinned people.

Some skin diseases are treated with light. For example, ultraviolet light can help heal a skin disease called "psoriasis," which makes the skin sore and flaky. The patient takes a special drug, then is exposed to ultraviolet light. The light treatment often can make the skin seem normal.

Ultraviolet light with wavelengths shorter than 300 nanometers can kill germs. Hospitals use intense "germicidal" lamps in hallways, operating rooms, laboratories, and intensive care units. They help stop the spread of infection, but they must be used carefully because the ultraviolet light can cause sunburn and other problems.

Laser Medicine

Doctors got into line early when lasers first came on the market. Light affects the skin and the eye most, so it should not be surprising that the first physicians to get lasers were eye and skin specialists (ophthalmologists and dermatologists). Other specialists soon became interested in lasers. Some surgeons sought a tool better than a knife for some tough operations. These pioneering physicians found lasers could cut tissue and do many other things—but not everything.

LASERS VS BLINDNESS

One of the laser's most important medical uses is to attack diabetic retinopathy, the leading cause of blindness in Americans between 20 and 64, which was mentioned in Chapter 4. It occurs in people who suffer from diabetes, a condition that prevents their bodies from digesting sugar properly. The vision of some diabetics as young as in their twenties can start to fade slowly away as blood, leaking from diseased blood vessels on their retinas, blocks the light.

Until the 1960s, medicine could do little to stop diabetic retinopathy. Then Dr. Francis L'Esperance began aiming laser beams into diabetic eyes. He found that carefully controlled pulses of visible laser light could slow the formation of the leaky blood vessels and slow the fading of vision. Other ophthalmologists confirmed that diabetics were helped by visible light from argon- or krypton-gas lasers. The treatment is not infallible; many diabetics still go blind. The laser can help them keep their vision longer than they otherwise could, however. Millions of diabetics have been treated in this way.

The simple treatment is done in the doctor's office, as shown in Figure 11–1. I watched one patient treated at the Massachusetts Eye and Ear Infirmary in Boston. The doctor fired about a hundred pulses of light into his eye, making tiny scars on the retina. A few patients feel a little

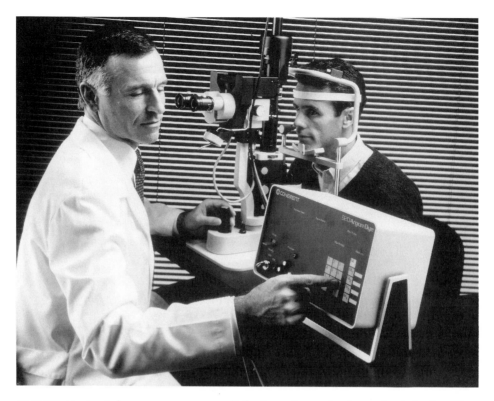

FIGURE 11–1 *A laser system treats diabetic retinopathy in a physician's office. (Courtesy of Coherent, Inc.)*

pain, but most feel nothing. The bright light dazzles their eyes, but they get up and walk away afterward as if they had only had an eye exam.

Another laser treatment can help people recover from an eye problem common in older people, cataracts. A cataract occurs when the eye's natural lens becomes cloudy, usually with age. Eye specialists can remove the cloudy lens and replace it with a plastic implant. They actually scoop out the lens material, leaving behind a filmy layer to hold fluid in the eyeball. Sometimes that layer can become cloudy after the cataract is removed, cutting off vision again. A very short pulse of laser light, focused to a tiny spot, can break that layer and let the patient see again, as shown in Figure 11–2. The doctor can do the job in his office, without cutting into the eye, and the patient's vision can return almost immediately. Doctors tell of patients who almost jumped for joy.

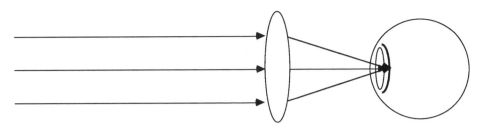

Laser pulse zaps cloudy membrane and breaks it

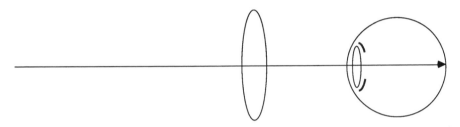

After laser pulse, the membrane opens and the patient can see

FIGURE 11–2 *A laser pulse, focused to a tiny point, can break a cloudy membrane in the eye and let a patient see clearly again.*

LASERS AND THE SKIN

The laser's biggest success in treating skin disease is in bleaching away dark birthmarks called "port-wine stains" because of their dark red color. They often appear on the face or neck, caused by extra blood vessels just beneath the surface. Regular surgery doesn't work well because the birthmark is spread over a large area. The best solution is to scan a visible laser beam over the surface.

The usual treatment is shining the blue-green beam from an argon laser onto the birthmark, which absorbs enough laser energy to burn and blister. Doctors treat a small area at a time and find that when the burn heals, the birthmark usually is much fainter. Specialists at Boston University Hospital and the Candela Corporation in Wayland, Massachusetts, have a new treatment that uses a dye laser, which—unlike most other lasers—has an adjustable wavelength. They match the dye laser's wavelength to colors absorbed by the blood vessels but not by normal skin.

This concentrates the laser energy in the blood vessels, helping to close them off without burning the rest of the skin.

The new treatment promises to help young people with port-wine stains. The birthmarks darken with age, and in young people they are not dark enough to treat with the argon laser—although they are dark enough to see. The new treatment also will avoid painful skin burns.

LASER SURGERY

Lasers will not replace the surgeon's traditional scalpel in all operations. For one thing, a surgical laser costs tens of thousands of dollars, far more than a knife. Also, knives are much better for some types of surgery, such as making large, deep cuts or sawing bones. However, lasers also have special strengths, in performing delicate surgery or removing thin layers of diseased cells.

The most common surgical laser is the carbon-dioxide laser, which emits infrared light at 10,600 nanometers. That wavelength is a big advantage because it is strongly absorbed by water—and the body is about 90 percent water. If the laser beam is focused down to a small spot, it can heat water so much that living cells vaporize without hurting the cells underneath them. The infrared beam can remove one layer of cells after another.

The laser also seals small blood vessels, *cauterizing* the wound to stop it from bleeding. Preventing blood loss makes it easier for the surgeon to see where to cut, and helps speed the patient's recovery.

Another advantage of the laser is that it can be focused onto a tiny spot to perform delicate *microsurgery*. Even the most sure-handed surgeon can have trouble moving a knife in tight places. A beam of light can reach where no knife can go.

What does this mean? The laser makes some otherwise risky surgery much safer. Suppose a person has a tiny cancer, a millimeter across, on the vocal cords. It is hard for a surgeon to remove that cancer with a knife, and the operation easily could cost the patient his voice. A laser makes such delicate surgery much easier and safer. The surgeon can focus the laser beam on the cancer and vaporize it. Because the laser light does not penetrate deeply, it does not damage the vocal cords. The same holds true in other types of surgery.

NEW LASER MEDICINE

Laser medicine is moving much too fast to cover it all here. Several new laser treatments are being developed, although not all may prove practical. These include:

• Laser photodynamic therapy for cancer, in which patients take doses of a dye that is held by cancer cells more than by other cells. After three days, the doctor zaps the cancer with a laser beam. When the dye absorbs the laser light, it breaks up, producing chemicals that kill the cancer cells. It has been tested on people and animals.

• Shattering of kidney stones with laser pulses. Some people build up hard "stones" in their kidneys, which can be very painful because there is no way to get them out. A laser beam can be sent through an optical fiber into the kidney, aimed at the stone. The energy from the laser pulses can shatter the stone into tiny enough fragments to pass freely from the body.

• Cleaning fatty clots out of arteries with laser energy passed through optical fibers. These clots are dangerous because they can block blood flow to vital organs. A blocked artery to the heart can cause a heart attack. A clogged artery to the leg can make the leg useless. Scientists have shown that laser light can help break up the clot if it heats a metal tip on the fiber or if the laser light directly hits the clot. They now are working on controlling the laser energy, so it does not accidentally make dangerous holes in the wall of the artery.

Reading and Writing
with Light

Light is information as well as life. Light lets you read the words on this page. Your eyes and your brain detect patterns on the paper and decode them as words. Both the seeing and the decoding are vital. You couldn't read this page if the room was dark or if the words were printed in a language you didn't know.

Machines also can read with light. Earlier, we talked about light detection and robot vision. Here, we will talk about machines made to read specific things, such as words on a page or special symbols. Some of those symbols are special codes, made to be easy for machines to read but not printed in any language that we know.

Light can write as well as read, and not just in photography or copying machines. Lasers can write computer data onto paper or special optical disks. I used a computer and a laser printer to make many of the drawings in this book.

Optical Character Readers

Earlier we saw how a simple robot could read the letter T. It compared the pattern it saw with a pattern stored in its memory. If the patterns matched, it recognized the letter. Devices called "optical character readers" work much like that, comparing what they see with patterns in the memory of an internal computer.

The internal workings of optical character readers differ, but they share many features. They scan the printed page, converting light reflected from the page into an electronic signal and decoding that signal to learn the pattern on the page. Then they compare the pattern with letter patterns in memory to "read" the printed words.

This sounds much easier than it is. The reader must adjust itself to read letters at different angles, of different sizes, and with different spacings. It also can't read all kinds of printing. Printers use many different typefaces. This book is printed in a typeface called Optima. Look at other books and at magazines and newspapers. Some use type that looks almost the same. Others look very different. You can read the letters of any typeface, but a machine cannot. If it's looking for a *T* with a plain bar across the top, it won't recognize one with little lines on the end of the bar, as shown in Figure 12–1. The fancier letter doesn't match the pattern in the machine's memory, so the machine doesn't know it's a *T*. Even if the machine knows what letters to look for, it may have trouble telling them apart. Most print is made to look pleasing to the human eye, not to be easy for machines to read.

Like people, optical character readers find it harder to decipher handwriting than printed words. Even hand printing can be difficult. One person's *n* may look like another's *h,* and the letters also can differ in size, slant, and spacing. Usually if people have to print something for optical character reading, they are given guidelines for printing letters and numbers.

Optical character reading (OCR) works best if words are printed in a type designed just for that purpose. A standardized OCR type is shown in Figure 12–2. It may look strange to human eyes, but it is easier for the machine to understand than the type in the rest of this book. A good optical character reader can read 19,999 out of every 20,000 letters in

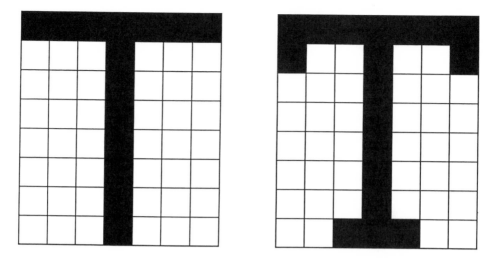

FIGURE 12–1 *You know these two patterns are both the letter T, but an optical character reader looking for the one on the left would not recognize the letter on the right as a T.*

that format. It can't read most of the rest, and it reads the wrong letter only once every 200,000 letters—if nobody's smudged the letters with greasy fingerprints.

Reading Bar Codes

OCR letters are a compromise. They let people and machines read the same words on paper, but they look odd to the human eye and are far from ideal for the electronic one. Suppose that there was no need for people to read the code. Then you could use other symbols that machines could read more easily than the alphabet.

Look on some of your mail, on magazines, or on food pacakges, and you'll see those machine-readable symbols. They are series of stripes, which people in the industry call a "bar code." The stripes are codes for letters and numbers. If a machine scans a spot of light straight

ISBN 0-684-18879-1

FIGURE 12–2 *A sample of OCR type*

across them, the reflected light is either "on" (white areas) or "off" (dark areas). That's the easiest type of code for optical detectors to read.

Some bar-code readers come in "wands" or "light pens" that a person holds. Store clerks run such wands over bar-coded price tags to read item numbers and prices into computers. A warehouse worker might use a similar wand to "read" the contents of a box directly into a computer, without punching keys, checking a list, or even reading a word himself.

There are many kinds of bar codes. You may have seen simple bar codes on the bottom of envelopes. The Postal Service puts them there as they process letters at major post offices. The little bars spell out your Zip Code to machines that sort the mail much faster than people.

The postal bar code is a simple one. Most others are more complex and carry more information. The codes usually are stripes of different width and equal height, such as the one in Figure 12–3. That code should look familiar. It's the Universal Product Code (UPC), and it's printed on most things you buy in the supermarket. Many bar codes are adapted from the Universal Product Code, which was developed for use in supermarkets and has since spread to many other industries. Its meaning is explained in the box in Figure 12–3.

The idea of automating supermarket checkout goes back to the early 1970s, when stores decided that it cost too much to mark prices on each package, keep inventory, and ring up purchases by hand. They decided to print standard codes on each package that could be read automatically. When the code was read into the store's computer, it would ring up the item's price.

The code had to be printed on metal or paper at the same time as the rest of the label. It had to be readable quickly and accurately from any angle. The engineers who designed the system picked the bar code you see on packages today. The stripes are more complex than you think. They automatically align the reader as well as identifying the item.

The codes are read with a thin red beam from a low-power helium-neon gas laser. The laser is mounted under the checkout counter, along with a light detector and electronics. When the clerk moves an item over a window in the counter, the laser beam turns on and scans a pattern designed to read bar codes from any angle. The light detector senses only the red laser light reflected from the moving package, and the electronics are programmed to recognize the pattern of light reflected from the bar code. Once the scanner has read the code, it tells the store computer, which returns the price, adds it to the customer's bill, and prints the register tape.

Scanners save time and money for large stores. A clerk needs less time to move a package over the window than to push buttons to enter a

---

FIGURE 12–3

0   12345 67890   5

The Universal Product Code. The bars in the Universal Product Code (UPC) encode the numbers printed at the bottom. The symbol encodes the twelve numbers printed with it and includes pairs of stripes at the ends and in the middle to help the scanner read it. The digit at the left identifies the type of product.

    0: Most products, including magazines, with a standard number

    2: Meat, vegetables, and other items sold at different weights

    3: Drugs and related items

    4: Products marked by the store

    5: Coupons

    6 or 7: Industrial products not sold through retail stores

The next five digits are a number assigned to each manufacturer, such as the Campbell Soup Company. The second five digits identifies the item, so each type of Campbell soup has a different number. The single digit at the right is used to check that the scanner has read the numbers correctly. The black and white stripes spell out those numbers to the scanner. The stripes that seem to be different widths really are groups of stripes. A wide dark stripe is two, three, or four single stripes joined together. (The scanner can read the stripes even if they are not separate.) The code has seven dark or white stripes for each number. The numbers do not have the same stripe codes on the right and left sides of the UPC symbol. This lets the scanner tell if it is reading the code forward or backward, so clerks don't have to line up labels for the scanner under the checkout counter. (Code copyright Uniform Code Council, Inc.; not for commercial reproduction) price by hand. Scanners also help the store manager keep track of what is in stock. For example, if the store started with 100 cans of tomato soup, and 90 have been sold, the manager knows how many cans remain—and the computer can automatically order more. Before scanners, someone had to count the cans on the shelf.

If you look carefully, you can see the laser light. It draws red lines on packages moving over the window. You can hold something still to see the pattern better. You don't see the beam come up from the window because it travels in a straight line to the package. It reaches your eye only if something reflects it. You can see a laser beam in a dusty or smoky room, because the dust or smoke reflects light to your eye, just as you sometimes can see sunbeams by light reflected from dust in the air.

Laser scanners worked so well in supermarkets that they are being used in many other places. The government uses similar bar codes to keep track of items in its warehouses. Companies that distribute magazines and paperback books also use such codes. Most magazines and books sold on newsstands have a UPC symbol on their front or back cover. Magazine distributors use scanners to read those symbols and count the number of magazines sold.

Laser Disks

Optical character readers work with letters that people can see and read. Bar-code scanners also work with symbols we can see, though most of us can't understand the codes. However, there are other ways that light can read information. For example, light can pack a lot of computer data onto a small optical disk.

To understand how optical storage works, let's look a minute at how computers store information. Data comes in units called "bits." One bit can be either a zero or one, on or off. Other information can be coded in bits, or "digitally" as engineers say (because the bits are a series of numbers). For example, in one standard code, 1000001 means capital *A*, and 1100001 means lowercase *a*. You can even code levels of speech in bits. When the computer is done with the data, the bits can be translated back into a form that people understand.

How small can a stored bit be? That depends on how you read and write it. You can focus a laser beam to a spot smaller than 1000 nanometers (a thousandth of a millimeter), so bits could be that size. A light spot might mean zero, and a dark spot one. You could squeeze a hundred million of those bits into a square centimeter. You can store optical data on a card, but more often it is stored on a disk, which spins like a phonograph record, but much faster.

There are several types of laser disk players. The one you are most likely to have heard of is the compact disk player, which plays music stored as a digital code on a shiny disk.

The making of a compact disk starts with converting music into a digital code. A laser beam then writes that code as tiny pits on a master disk. (The writing laser has much higher power than the laser that later reads the disks.) That pattern of holes is pressed into clear plastic disks. Then the plastic is coated with a thin layer of shiny aluminum and a protective plastic coating. The pattern of holes remains fixed in the aluminum layer as pits in the shiny surface.

The disks are played by focusing a semiconductor laser beam onto the aluminum layer, as shown in Figure 12–4. The pits reflect light differently than the rest of the aluminum layer. A sensor measures those differences, and electronics decode the signal to tell what is on the disk.

Compact disks are popular because their digital coding makes the music clean and sharp. Scratches and smudges on their surface are out of focus, so they don't spoil the music, as they do on phonograph records. Compact disks are only twelve centimeters (4¾ inches) in diameter, much smaller than a standard thirty-centimeter (12-inch) phonograph record, but they can play a much broader range of tones, and one side can hold twice as much music as one side of a phonograph record.

Look at a compact disk, and the first thing you are likely to see is a rainbow of colors. You see that rainbow because the tiny data pits are lined up in rings that act like a diffraction grating. You can see the thin lines that seem to run in circles. Those are the lines of pits—too small to see by themselves—that scatter the light to make the spectrum.

The same idea is used to store television pictures on videodisks. Videodisks are larger than compact disks, usually thirty centimeters (twelve inches) across, and the players work a little differently. However, the basic idea is very similar. In fact, optical disk technology was origi-

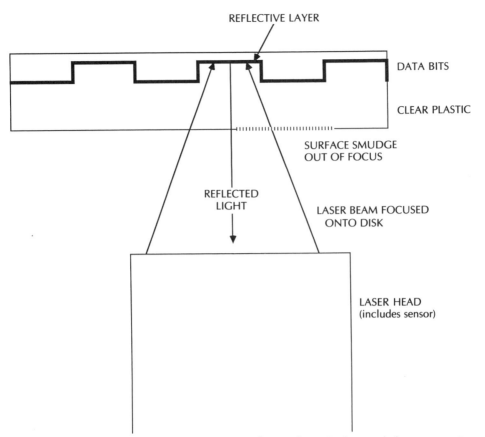

FIGURE 12–4 *The beam from a semiconductor laser is focused down to a tiny spot to play music from the spots on a compact disk.*

nally made for videodisks, but videodisks did not sell well, and it was adapted for other uses.

Can computers read the digital data stored on compact disks? They can, in a sense. The bits on regular compact disks contain music, which doesn't mean anything to a computer. However, the compact disk format can store computer data in what's called a "CD-ROM," for compact disk, read-only memory. One CD-ROM can store 600 million bytes (each byte is eight bits), about a thousand times more than the floppy disks used with personal computers. The Grolier Educational Corporation published the text (but not the pictures) of an encyclopedia on a single CD-ROM—and had room left over!

So far, we have talked only about reading data stored on optical disks. However, if the disk is coated with a material sensitive to light, you can write data as well. Compact disks and CD-ROMs are not sensitive to light, but other types of optical disks are.

Optical data also can be stored on cards coated with light-sensitive materials. Blue Cross/Blue Shield of Maryland stores medical histories of people who carry its insurance policies on such cards. People carry the cards with them. A doctor can plug the card into a reader to find out such things as drug allergies and how to bill the patient.

Writing with Light

Light can write as well as read. All it takes is a surface that changes when light strikes it. Earlier we talked about photographic film and copying machines. Light can write on both of them.

Printers use light to make master copies of type, like the words used in this book. Light writes each letter onto a photographic film. Sometimes the light is a bulb shining through a stencil; sometimes the light is a laser beam scanning the pattern of the letter. That master copy can be copied photographically and used to make "printing plates" that put the black ink on the white paper. There are many different types of printing, but in most of them light helps the printer transfer the image from one stage to the next.

Laser Printers

A copying machine works by transferring an image of the original to a light-sensitive drum. Suppose that we want to write directly onto the drum, without bothering with an original. We could use a laser beam to write a pattern, spell out words, and draw pictures. Then the drum could transfer the image to paper. That's how a laser printer works.

The printer turns the laser beam off and on as it scans the drum. Where the page is supposed to be white, the laser comes on and discharges the drum surface. Where the paper is to be black, the laser beam is switched off, and the drum keeps its charge. The charged areas of the drum collect toner, and transfer the toner to paper. The idea is shown in Figure 12–5.

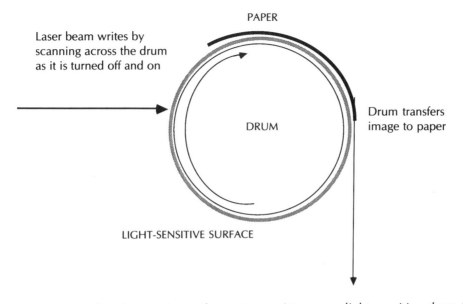

PAPER

Laser beam writes by
scanning across the drum
as it is turned off and on

DRUM

Drum transfers
image to paper

LIGHT-SENSITIVE SURFACE

FIGURE 12–5 *In a laser printer, the pattern written on a light-sensitive drum is transferred to paper as in a copying machine.*

Laser printers work much like copying machines because they are built by the same companies, using the same technology. The first laser printers were very expensive but very fast. When they came out in 1975, they cost $300,000 and printed over a hundred pages a minute. You can buy a slow laser printer for under $2000 now, but fast laser printers are still expensive. You probably have seen their work in your mailbox. High-speed laser printers generate most of the form letters that are addressed to you by name.

Most laser printers are used by businesses with personal computers. They have become very popular because they print quickly and well. A laser printer can print out a page that looks almost as good as a typewritten original in a matter of seconds—much faster than "letter-quality" printers. They can squeeze 300 dots per inch, two to four times as many as a mechanical dot-matrix printer. They are so good that I used a laser printer to make many of the drawings in this book, including the picture of one in Figure 12–5.

Light at Work

Light can do more than read or write. It does many jobs in industry and elsewhere. Some jobs just involve seeing, such as that of a factory inspector checking for defects. Others are more complex. Light can make delicate measurements, and it can draw straight lines for construction workers.

Earlier we saw that concentrated light energy can set things on fire or perform surgery. It also can drill, cut, and weld in industry. Lasers do industrial jobs ranging from drilling holes in baby-bottle nipples to welding seals on batteries and heart pacemakers. Light works at too many jobs for us to list here, but we can tell you about some of its more interesting tasks.

Making Straight Lines

We take straight lines for granted, but it isn't easy to draw one. Compare a line you draw by hand with the edge of a ruler. Or try to draw a long line with a short ruler. Straight lines are big problems for builders. If their lines aren't straight, a building might tilt. Builders haven't always found it easy to draw straight lines. In most houses built before the 1900s, it's hard to find walls that are straight and meet at right angles.

When you try to draw straight lines, you soon find that no ruler is long enough and no tape measure is straight enough. You need something that can be as long as you want but still perfectly straight and flexible enough to fit inside any room. That sounds like a job for a beam of light.

Contractors use a helium-neon laser. Its red beam makes a small, bright spot or narrow line that is easy for workmen to see. The laser can help workmen align things to keep them straight. A laser plane generator can draw a straight, level line all around a room. It contains a rotating prism head that sweeps the laser beam in a circle, drawing a line at the same level. That laser-drawn line tells where to put framing for a suspended ceiling, making the job much easier—and more accurate—than it would be by hand.

Laser lines also can help farmers prepare fields for irrigation. If water is to flow evenly, the field must be smooth, with no high or low points. A farmer can set a laser line at a slight angle to mark the grade he wants on the field. Then he attaches a sensing system to the blade of a grader. The sensor moves the blade up and down, so it is at the height the farmer wants to give the field the proper slant. This makes sure that the field gets the right amount of water, making irrigation more efficient. Similar laser tools help road builders grade highways.

Surveying

Surveying is measurement of the height and location of points on the earth's surface. Surveyors measure the size of a plot of land, help plan the design of buildings, and help decide the paths of roads and water lines. The art of surveying is an old one; it was one of George Washington's early jobs.

Surveyors have long taken *sightings* to measure land. One standard way of surveying is called "triangulation." The surveyor measures the length of one side of a triangle with a tape measure. Then he measures the angles between the end points of that line and the third point of the triangle. After measuring all the angles, the surveyor can calculate how long the other sides are without measuring them. One of those calculated lines then can serve as the known side of another triangle.

Surveyors measure angles with a small telescope. First they look at one point, then turn the telescope to look at a second. Their instrument, called a "transit," or "theodolite," measures how much the telescope turned between the two points.

The laser is another powerful tool for measuring distances too long for a tape measure. The surveyor can send a short pulse of laser light to a target at the point to be measured. The target reflects the light back to the instrument, which measures how long the light took to make the round trip. Multiplying the time by the speed of light gives the distance, as shown in Figurre 13–1. Radar works the same way but uses microwaves.

Remote Sensing and Infrared Thermography

Because light travels through the air, you can use it to measure things far away. This is called "remote sensing." A television camera in a satellite is a remote sensor, looking down on the earth from far above. So is a camera in an airplane. A remote sensor also could be in a van looking at smoke coming from tall chimneys a few kilometers away or on the ground looking at clouds far above the earth's surface.

Many remote sensors are built to make specific measurements. Suppose, for example, we wanted to see what parts of the earth's surface

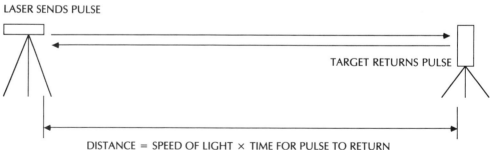

LASER SENDS PULSE

TARGET RETURNS PULSE

DISTANCE = SPEED OF LIGHT × TIME FOR PULSE TO RETURN

FIGURE 13–1 *Distance can be measured by timing how long it takes a laser pulse to make a round trip.*

were covered by plants. We could build a remote sensor to look for wavelengths reflected strongly by chlorophyll but only weakly by dirt, sand, and water. Parts of the earth covered with plants would be bright at that wavelength, while the oceans and bare land would be darker.

Satellite remote sensors often take pictures of the ground and relay the pictures back to Earth where people can study them. Weather forecasters use satellite photos to help predict the paths of storms and tomorrow's weather. Map-makers use satellite and airplane photos to make new maps and improve old ones. Military analysts use such photos to try to figure out what other countries are doing.

Scientists also use remote sensing. For example, they might build a laser system that emits light at a wavelength where an air pollutant absorbs light strongly. By firing those laser pulses into the air and seeing what light returns to their sensors, they can see where the pollution is.

Another example of remote sensing is called "thermography." As we learned earlier, the hotter something is, the more infrared light it emits. Thermography uses this to measure temperatures by looking at the amount of infrared light emitted, the wavelengths emitted, or both. Thermography helps engineers find where heat leaks out of buildings.

Interferometry

Earlier we saw how light waves could interfere with each other. Two waves of the same wavelength cancel if the peak of one comes at the same point as the valley of the other. They add together if the peaks and valleys line up. Such interference lets optical engineers measure distances smaller than a wavelength of light.

Figure 13–2 shows an example of how this works. Two flat plates are placed next to each other, but one is tilted. The back plate reflects all light; the front one reflects some and transmits some. The whole area gets light from a single laser. If light passes through the first plate and is reflected by the second, it travels twice the distance between the plates before coming back to meet the light wave reflected at the first plate. (You can check that by tracing with your finger on the drawing.) If the two plates are half a wavelength apart, light reflected from the back plate has traveled a full wavelength more than the light reflected from the front

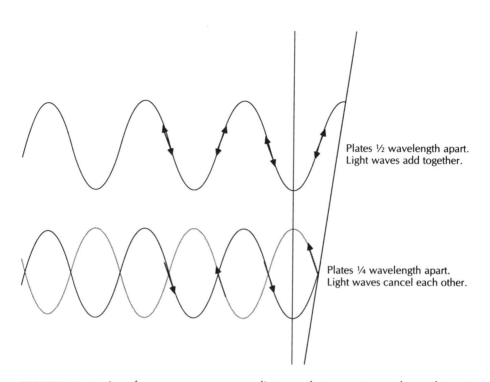

FIGURE 13–2 *Interference measures a distance between two glass plates to within a quarter the wavelength of light. The waves at top combine because the wave reflected from the back plate adds to the wave reflected from the front one. Those at the bottom cancel because the wave reflected from the back plate is out of phase with the one reflected from the front plate.*

plate. The two waves are in phase—their peaks are at the same point—so they add together.

At another point, the two plates are a quarter wavelength apart. That means that light reflected from the back plate travels half a wavelength more, and is out of phase with the other light. The peak of one wave is at the trough of the other, and the two cancel out.

If you were looking at these two laser-lighted plates, you would see a set of light and dark stripes, the light stripes where the light waves add, and the dark stripes where they cancel. The stripes are called interference fringes. If you know the wavelengths of the light, you can measure the distance between the two plates. Each pair of stripes (one light, one dark) measures one-half wavelength. If you're using the 633-

nanometer red wavelength of the helium-neon laser, that pair of stripes measures about 300 nanometers, or 0.0003 millimeter.

Who needs such precise measurements? As might seem fitting, the makers of optics do, because many optical surfaces must be accurate to within a fraction of a wavelength of light. They are not the only ones, however. In a surprising number of cases, accuracy to a thousandth of a millimeter can be vital.

Holographic Measurements

Earlier we saw that holography could make three-dimensional images. Holography isn't just making pretty pictures. It also is put to practical use in industrial measurements.

Suppose you want to watch very carefully how something changes under pressure or how it behaves when it's vibrating. For example, suppose a machine is vibrating and you want to find out what part is moving the most. Your eye can't see the motion, but there is a way to spot it.

The trick is to take two holograms of the machine, very close together in time, then look at the 3-D image. You need light from a special laser that produces two short pulses, perhaps a millionth of a second apart. Each pulse takes a hologram at that instant, and both are recorded on the same piece of film. When laser light shines on the hologram to form a three-dimensional image of the machine, it is covered with interference fringes. Those fringes show where and how much the machine moved between laser pulses.

This is called holographic interferometry, and it also tests for weakness in airplane tires. In the tire tests, something happens between laser pulses: air is pumped into the tire. If the tire is good, the fringe pattern should be even over the whole tire. If the tire has a defect, it shows up as an unusual pattern of fringes in one area of the tire, as in Figure 13–3.

Laser Drilling

The ancients knew that light could make things burn if they put enough light in the right place. However, it was hard to concentrate a lot of energy in one place until the laser came along.

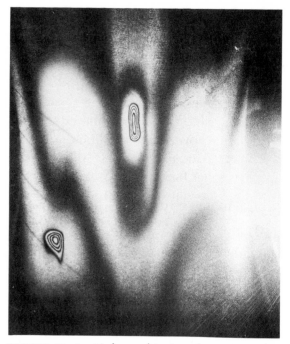

FIGURE 13–3 *Holographic interferometry pinpoints a flaw in an airplane tire. This view is from inside the tire. (Courtesy of Newport Corp.)*

Theodore Maiman's first laser was so tiny it could fit in one hand. Soon there were bigger and more powerful lasers. Laser researchers aimed the beams at things and found that they could punch holes in some of them. For a while, they jokingly measured laser power in "gillettes," the number of razor blades they could drill through with a single pulse. It was not long before they put lasers to work drilling holes.

How can a beam of light drill a hole? It heats the material. First the laser energy melts the surface. Then it vaporizes the liquid. All this happens very fast. Drilling laser pulses last only billionths of a second. That speed is important, because it keeps the laser energy where the hole is being drilled. Laser energy that arrived more slowly could spread through the material, heating all of it a little. Short pulses drill holes by heating only a little material to very high temperatures.

One early use of lasers was drilling holes in diamond, which is the hardest material known. Diamond tools are so hard they can cut any other material, and they withstand wear very well. One use of diamonds is in making thin wires. The metal is pulled or drawn through a hole in a diamond *die*. Before the laser, it was hard to drill the holes in diamond. Unlike other tools, a laser beam isn't dulled by the hard diamond, so it can drill through the die. Lasers also drill holes in many other hard materials, such as metals used inside jet engines.

Lasers also are very good at drilling soft materials. You might not think you need a laser for soft materials. However, it is not easy to make tiny holes at just the right places. You'll understand if you try to punch holes in Jell-O with a thin straw. The softer the material, the more likely it is to move. The harder you push, the more it will move. Another problem is that the thin drills (often more like pins than drills) are likely to break, even in a soft material.

A laser beam avoids those problems. Nothing touches the soft material to bend it out of shape. The laser beam can't break off; it just keeps punching holes. That's why you probably met your first laser-drilled hole long ago. For many years, lasers have drilled the holes in most baby-bottle nipples.

Lasers also drill holes in paper and other soft materials. Why would anyone drill holes in paper? The paper is cigarette paper, and the holes let air flow smoothly through it to help control how much tar and nicotine are in the smoke.

Laser Marking

A hole need not go all the way through to be useful. If you want to put a peg into a hole, you may not want the hole to go through the board. You might want a hole as a mark or decoration. Lasers can do that job, too.

Suppose, for example, you are making car engines, and you want to put a serial number on each one. The number must stay on the engine, even when it is covered with grease and grime (look at an old car engine if you *really* want to see something dirty). Ink couldn't do that. You also want to write the numbers as fast as possible, because time on the assembly line is too expensive for someone to carve numbers into the engine.

A laser marker can solve the problem. The laser fires short, powerful pulses that make small holes in the metal. The beam moves between each pulse, making a series of holes that spell out the serial number. In seconds, the laser has done the job and is marking the next engine.

Lasers also can mark thin metal sheets that would bend if you hammered numbers into them.

Lasers can mark patterns as well as dots. Suppose you wanted to put a symbol on a metal case to show your company made it. You could make a stencil-like *mask,* with the mark cut out. Then you fire laser pulses through it, focusing the pattern onto the surface you want to mark. The laser light writes the image of the pattern. It works faster if you coat the surface with black paint to absorb light efficiently.

Laser markings can be decorations, too. Some companies use lasers to engrave patterns in wood or other materials. You may find laser-etched pens or wooden plaques in gift shops. The laser can make those patterns much faster than a workman with carving tools.

Cutting with a Laser

The energy in a laser beam can cut as well as drill. The basic idea is much the same, although the details are different. In laser cutting, heat is deposited more slowly and the cut is made differently. The laser energy heats the material, but often the hot material burns in the air before it can evaporate.

A close look at laser cutting can show the difference. A laser metal cutter blows air at the cut, so there is always plenty of oxygen to combine with the hot metal in the cutting area. You sometimes can see vivid signs of the way cuts are made. I have a piece of laser-cut three-quarter-inch plywood on which the cuts are black with soot.

Laser cutting works best for thin materials. Sometimes lasers cut such ordinary materials as paper and cloth. What can a laser do better than scissors? One thing is to cut patterns in expensive cloth, such as the material used in men's suits. A computer calculates how to cut the cloth so most of it ends up in suits, not as scraps on the floor. Then a laser beam traces those patterns to cut the cloth. The laser follows the computer-calculated lines better than a knife or scissors, working faster and without the risk of snagging the cloth. The laser beam is much more powerful than those used for measurement—dozens of watts—but not nearly so powerful as needed for other types of cutting. Lasers also can cut out fancy patterns in paper, usually for things like greeting cards.

Lasers also cut harder materials used to build airplanes. Like clothes, airplanes are made of many different-shaped pieces, which must be cut in special shapes and put together. A computer can arrange those pieces on a sheet of metal or other material. Then a carbon-dioxide laser can cut them out.

Actually, lasers only cut some materials used in building airplanes. Most planes are made of aluminum, a soft metal that strongly reflects the 10,000-nanometer wavelength of the carbon-dioxide laser. Because it is soft and absorbs very little laser energy, aluminum is easier to cut with a saw. Lasers are better for other materials used in high-performance planes. Among those is titanium, a metal that is very hard to cut with a saw and that absorbs much more light at 10,000 nanometers than aluminum. Lasers also are good at cutting light and strong nonmetallic "composite" materials, made of glues, plastics, and fabrics, used in some newer planes.

Many other materials are cut with lasers, including plastics, rubber, glass, wood, and metals. However, some things do not cut well with lasers. Laser engineers joke about experiments that failed, such as trying to cut fish and finding that the laser had cooked the fish while it cut.

Ray Guns and Reality: Light at War

Some people have called the laser "the light fantastic." They mean that the laser can do marvelous things, but there is another type of fantasy about the laser. Too often people confuse the real-world laser with the ray gun of fantasy and science fiction.

Soldiers sometimes do use lasers, but not as weapons. Today, real lasers can point out targets to "smart bombs" or missiles, or they can be used in mock battles. Perhaps someday lasers will be used as weapons, but even then they won't be the pocket blasters you see on television.

Light Weapons and Death Rays

The idea of using light as a weapon goes back at least to ancient Greek times. We don't know if it's true that Archimedes used mirrors to set Roman ships on fire 2200 years ago, but the legend does tell us that people thought about it.

When people began writing science fiction, they began dreaming up futuristic weapons. In 1896, H. G. Wells wrote *The War of the Worlds*, in which Martians invaded the earth. He equipped the Martians with a terrible weapon, a "heat ray," which set on fire everything that it touched. Wells had a good imagination, but that weapon had a scientific basis. It was a powerful beam of infrared light.

In the years that followed, scientists discovered X rays and nuclear radiation. At first, scientists didn't understand those types of radiation, and the science-fiction writers that followed Wells knew much less than the scientists. They imagined "death rays" that killed or paralyzed on contact. Unlike the bulky heat rays used by Wells' Martians, these ray guns could fit easily in the hero's pocket, just like a six-shooter in a cowboy's holster. They bore little relation to physical reality, but they nicely filled the needs of the story.

When the laser came along, it sounded so much like a ray gun that many science-fiction writers picked up the new word. The laser could indeed pack a powerful burst of light energy in a narrow beam. As we saw in the last chapter, it wasn't long before lasers were punching holes in razor blades and otherwise demonstrating impressive power. Articles about "the incredible laser" predicted that laser weapons were just around the corner. Scientists were more cautious about laser weapons, and time has proved them right.

Why aren't lasers death rays? Because they emit ordinary light. Light has no magical power; it only deposits energy. The only way light can damage anything is if it is concentrated, as in a powerful laser beam. It can't kill or stun a person on contact; it can only burn a hole if it has enough energy. Ultraviolet light can kill germs or cause a bad sunburn, but doesn't pack enough energy to be lethal to people. X rays and gamma rays, which have high-energy photons, pack enough wallop to harm human cells but their damage to people is long-term, not sudden death.

Another problem is that small lasers do not store much energy. A laser pistol small enough to hold in your hand could not store enough energy to damage anything much larger than a fly. (Except for eyes, which are made to be very sensitive to light.) A laser pistol might be frightening, but an ordinary revolver would be a much better weapon.

Larger lasers store more energy, but as we've pointed out, the worst danger from laser beams is to the eyes. Powerful beams can burn the skin, but they are hardly lethal weapons. The biggest danger from the laser is not the beam that comes out the front end but the electrical power supply in the back that drives the laser. A few people have been killed when they put their fingers in the wrong place and were electrocuted.

Real Laser Weapons

Could lasers make real weapons? Military scientists are trying, but the answer to that question has to be "maybe."

It is fairly easy to make lasers that can damage the eye. A few people have accidentally zapped their eyes with laser beams and hurt their vision. If a short, powerful pulse of laser light hits the back of the eyeball, it can burn the retina and release drops of blood, leaving a scar and a blind spot on the retina. That impairs vision but does not leave the victim totally blind.

Nobody would admit to trying to make lasers to zap enemy eyeballs. However, military scientists *are* trying to target enemy sensors. The idea is to overload light sensors so they can't "see" to direct weapons. For example, some guided missiles are made to home in on infrared light, such as might come from hot airplane exhaust. Shining a laser beam at such a missile could dazzle its electronic eyes, the way looking into car headlights at night makes it hard to see the stars.

Other military scientists tried for years to make lasers powerful enough to destroy fast-moving targets on the battlefield, such as enemy missiles and helicopters. Traveling at the speed of light, a powerful laser beam could reach its target instantaneously. The U.S. Department of Defense spent about $2 billion studying such lasers but found very serious problems.

One problem is that a laser must be very large to be very powerful. Even a laser that filled most of an airplane the size of a passenger jet might not be big enough to do the job. The big lasers that were built did not work very well. Many highly trained technicians were needed to get them to work at all. That's hardly what you want on a battlefield, where weapons must work in rain and mud. Large optics that can withstand high powers also are hard to build. Other problems involved trying to hit moving targets. Once laser power reached the level needed to damage a target, the air could not transmit it well. To reword an old saying, a laser weapon couldn't hit the broad side of a barn. One wag joked that the only way to damage something with a laser weapon was to drop the laser on it!

Laser weapons are still being studied today, but for a different purpose: to defend against attack by nuclear missiles. The goal is to destroy missiles in space with high-energy laser beams. It is part of President Reagan's controversial Strategic Defense Initiative, or "Star Wars" program.

A huge laser might be put on a mountaintop, where it would be much easier to build, power, and service than in space. The beam would be aimed upward, to satellites carrying relay mirrors that would direct it around the world and focus the laser energy onto target missiles. Other possibilities include putting compact laser battle stations into orbit or having them poised on rockets ready for launch on warning of attack.

None of these ideas is ready to work tomorrow. The mountaintop laser seems the most realistic, but even that is years away from testing. Many questions remain about how well the beam could track and deliver laser energy to the target. Some scientists think such weapons could be built; others do not. Because the program involves sensitive political issues and billions of dollars, it is likely to remain controversial for years to come.

Laser Targeting Systems

Today's soldiers may not be armed with laser weapons, but lasers have been used on the battlefield for nearly two decades. They first saw action in the Vietnam War. They were used not as weapons but to help other weapons find their targets.

One simple battlefield use of lasers is to find the range to a target. Artillery officers firing shells need that information to tell how to aim their guns. Military laser rangefinders work much like those used in surveying. They send out a short pulse of light and time how long it takes to return.

A different laser system can mark or "designate" a target with a coded series of light pulses. A soldier aims the laser designator at a target, such as an enemy tank. Then a sensor in a missile or "smart bomb" homes in on the laser spot, which generally is invisible infrared light. This homing mechanism makes it much easier for missiles and bombs to hit their targets.

Some police departments and organizations like the Federal Bureau of Investigation use a different type of laser targeting system. They bolt a helium-neon laser onto a rifle and line up the laser with the rifle bore. The red laser spot points out where a bullet fired from the rifle would hit, making it much easier to aim the weapons.

Laser War Games

You might be surprised to learn that laser tag games weren't invented by toymakers. The idea came from a military system used in battle training called "MILES" for Modular Integrated Laser Engagement System.

Laser tag games aren't really played with lasers, but they use the same basic idea. Players wearing light sensors fire beams of light at each other. The sensors keep score, telling who's been hit by the light—even if the light itself is invisible.

The real military system does use lasers, but only low-power semiconductor lasers. The lasers are attached to weapons such as rifles and bazookas and fire pulses when soldiers pull the trigger. The pulses are coded and tell what type of weapon is "firing" them. Soldiers, tanks, and other battlefield equipment all wear sensors that watch for the laser pulses. To make the war games realistic, only certain weapons can "kill" certain targets. If laser pulses from a rifle hit a tank, nothing happens. But if it's hit by an antitank missile, the sensor tells the scorekeeper that the tank has been destroyed—and just to make sure, fires off a burst of purple smoke and disables the tank controls.

Sensors and Night Vision

The military services use many types of optical and infrared sensors on the battlefield. They also use infrared night-vision systems to see in the dark.

Many military night-vision systems work near the 10,000-nanometer wavelengths at which room-temperature objects emit black-body radiation. Soldiers can use them to spot the body heat of an enemy soldier hiding behind a (cooler) tree or to spot the heat from the engine of a tank.

Lighting Up the Future

This book has shown how our knowledge of light has grown. The ancients knew only a little about light. Nearly 400 years ago, Dutch spectacle-makers learned how to make simple telescopes and microscopes and opened new worlds to mankind. As we learned more about light, we were better able to use it, from lighting our homes to performing laser surgery.

People will continue learning about light. Thirty years ago this would have been a very different book. The laser was not yet invented, and fiber optics were newborn. More is coming. The next thirty years will bring exciting new developments in optics. We cannot predict them exactly, but we can point out some things to look for. If history is any guide, there are sure to be surprises.

Home Information Systems

Some new optical technology is well on the way. In Chapter 12, we saw that an optical disk could hold an encyclopedia's worth of words (although not all the pictures) with room to spare. Engineers are working on new optical disks that will be able to respond to your actions. The costs of optical disks are coming down. Some people believe that soon copies of a disk might cost as little as a dollar each to make.

What does all this mean? It could mean that before long a computerized information system will replace the printed encyclopedia. It would include a personal computer and an optical disk player and might work something like an automatic index. If you typed in *laser,* it could show the encyclopedia entry for *laser.* It also could show any other entries that contained the word *laser.* If the disk stored pictures, it could show a drawing of a laser on the screen.

Once you had the computer and the optical disk player, you might get other optical-disk references, such as an optical-disk almanac. If you wanted to look up the population of Montgomery, Alabama, you could type *population, Alabama, Montgomery,* and see it on the screen. You could buy other optical-disk references, from baseball records to *Who's Who.*

Optical disks also might store pictures, quizzes, or self-study courses. For example, the optical-disk almanac might have graphs plotting changes in city populations over the years. A self-study mathematics course could show you how to do problems, then test you on them. The disk would route you to the next problem after a right answer and review ideas after a wrong answer. What it reviewed would depend on what wrong answer you gave.

A computer with optical disks would not be a real robot teacher, but it could help you work on skills such as math and spelling.

Better Home Communications

In Chapter 10, we saw how fiber-optic communications are slowly spreading and will eventually reach homes. Why is this important? Because fiber optics can carry much more information than the wires that now bring telephone calls to your home. To understand what that means, we need to explain a bit more about how information is communicated.

Remember that information can be measured in units called "bits." Imagine that each bit is a drop of water. How much water we can get to a house depends on how big a pipe we use. Use a straw, and you get a dribble. If you want a lot, you need a big pipe.

Before fiber optics, people building communication systems had to work with straws and settle for bringing a dribble of information to homes. That wasn't bad if you only needed a dribble, like a single voice over the phone. But it meant you couldn't even think of other services. If water came to your house through a straw-sized pipe, you would have glasses to drink from, but you wouldn't think of showers or dishwashers.

Fiber optics let people think about more communications than telephones and cable television. Optical fibers have enough information capacity to handle videotelephones—telephones that send pictures as well as voices. They could handle computer data or new types of cable television. They could carry signals from gas and electric meters and almost anything else you could imagine. It's like being connected to a whole lake full of water after getting your water through a straw.

Japan, France, Canada, West Germany, and Great Britain have tested fiber-optic transmission to homes. Companies in the United States are interested, too. Don't expect fiber optics to come to your home tomorrow. It still costs too much, but prices are going down and people's communication needs are increasing. Fiber optics is the future of communications, but we're not sure when the future will come.

Optical Computers

Fiber optics and optical disks are here today and will be used more tomorrow. Other new ways for optics to handle information are just around the corner. Many fall under the vague heading of optical computing.

Today's computers are electronic and use semiconductor circuits to move electrons. Electronic computers are very good at some things. They can add a long list of numbers much faster than people. But they are not good at everything. As we saw earlier, they can't recognize pictures well. They also have trouble understanding speech (although they can *talk* easily, as you can hear in any toy store). They simply are not wired for those jobs.

Some scientists believe that optics can do those jobs better than electronics. Lenses and other optical devices handle light differently from the way electronics handle currents. An ordinary microcomputer chip can handle only one electrical input at a time. Yet many beams of light can pass through a lens at once.

What sort of things can an optical computer do? Most are too complicated to explain here. For example, they can easily solve some complex mathematical problems, but you won't understand what the problems mean unless you take advanced calculus in college. They also can clean up fuzzy photographs or recognize objects in a picture, although neither the cleaning up nor the pattern recognition are perfect.

Optical computing can do other things as well. One new idea is called "bistable optics." Bistable optical devices can be either transparent or dark. That is, sometimes they block light, and sometimes they let light through. You can control these devices to switch light signals, just as electronic circuits can switch electrical signals.

Scientists are working on many new optical devices that can switch or otherwise change the light passing through them. Someday these may be building blocks for other types of optical computers. Some scientists think optical computers someday will be a thousand times more powerful than today's electronic supercomputers.

Ultrafast Phenomena

Speed is one attraction of optical computing—and not just because no electron can ever move at the speed of light. The fastest man-made events are pulses of light. Scientists at American Telephone & Telegraph's Bell Laboratories have made pulses that last only six femtoseconds. That's six millionths of a billionth of a second, or 0.000,000,000,000,006 second. That clump of light contains only three waves and is about 1800 nanometers long.

Optical computers would not have to work that fast to outrace digital electronics, but those ultrafast pulses do show what is possible with light. They tell how fast you can turn light off and on again—important when communication signals must be switched from one place to another.

Ultrafast pulses also can be used to probe what happens in materials. For example, scientists want to learn how atoms and molecules combine. Ultrafast pulses of light can take "snapshots" of what is happening at any given instant.

New Telescopes

Optical computing and ultrafast phenomena are new fields, but big changes are coming in some traditional areas of optics. One of the most dramatic is in telescopes.

The past half century has seen great advances in most areas of optics. Yet it was more than half a century ago that work started on what is still the world's most productive large telescope, the 200-inch (5.08-meter) Hale telescope on Mount Palomar in southern California, shown

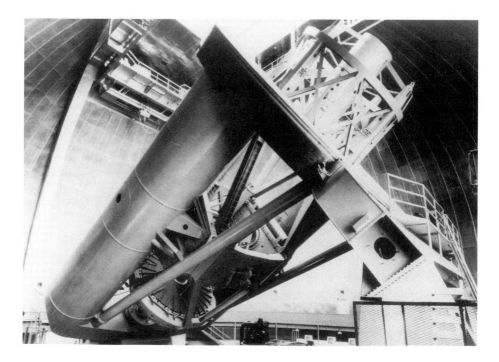

FIGURE 15–1 *The 200-inch (5.08-meter) Hale telescope at Mount Palomar Observatory in California. Still the world's most important working optical telescope, it was designed half a century ago. (Palomar Observatory Photograph)*

in Figure 15–1. The Great Depression and World War II slowed work on the telescope, and it did not begin operation until 1948. Yet it remains the "big gun" of the astronomical world. Only a single telescope is larger, a six-meter telescope in Mount Pastukhov in the Soviet Union, but that telescope has never worked well since it was first used in 1976.

What stalled the progress in building bigger telescopes was the same thing that hurt the Soviet six-meter telescope: massive mirrors present serious problems. It takes a long time for them to warm and cool, and inevitable changes in temperature distort the surface of the mirror. The changes are slight, but even a change of a fraction of a wavelength of light can hurt the optical quality of a mirror.

Solutions to the problem have emerged only recently. Astronomer Roger Angel, of the University of Arizona, has found a way to make lightweight mirrors eight meters in diameter. Such mirrors can be put together to make larger telescopes. Half a century after the Corning Glass Works cast the mirror for the Hale telescope, the size of ground-based telescopes is once again increasing.

The California Institute of Technology, which operates the Palomar Observatory, has teamed with the University of California to build the ten-meter Keck telescope on a Hawaiian mountaintop. The design for that giant telescope is shown in Figure 15–2. Three other American universities and an Italian research group are planning a giant binocular telescope, with a pair of eight-meter mirrors. And astronomers working with the National Science Foundation are planning a giant National New Technology telescope, fifteen meters in diameter.

Such giant telescopes on the ground will be superb at collecting light, but they cannot give us the sharpest view of the universe. The air bends light waves as they pass through it and blurs the images of stars. The blurring is invisible to our eyes, but it shows up in telescopes. (You can see a similar blurring if you look through clear water at a pattern in the bottom of a swimming pool or bathtub.)

The way around this problem is to put a telescope in orbit. That's why NASA has spent over a billion dollars building the Hubble space telescope, shown in Figure 15–3. At ninety-six inches (2.4 meters) in diameter, it is smaller than many telescopes on the ground. It can't collect as much light as the Hale telescope. But the light entering it will not

FIGURE 15–2 *The ten-meter Keck telescope is being built in Hawaii by the California Institute of Technology and the University of California. When complete, it will be the world's largest optical telescope. (Courtesy California Association for Research in Astronomy)*

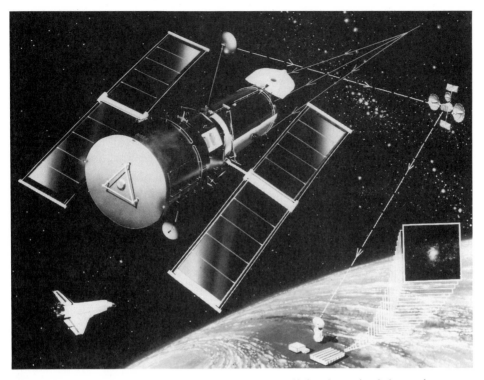

FIGURE 15–3 *The Hubble space telescope will be launched from the space shuttle. Although at 2.4 meters it is smaller than many telescopes on the ground, it will give us the clearest pictures ever of the universe because it does not have to look through air. (Courtesy National Aeronautics and Space Administration)*

be blurred by the air. Astronomers are eagerly awaiting its launch from the space shuttle, so they can get the clearest views yet of the universe.

Atomic Probes

We mentioned earlier that lasers can sense things like air pollutants. That is just part of a fast-growing field called "spectroscopy." Atoms and molecules absorb and emit light at certain wavelengths because of their internal structures. Because their internal structures and energy-level ladders differ, so do those wavelengths. That is, each atom or molecule absorbs and emits light at its own special wavelengths. That means that those wavelengths tell what atoms or molecules are present.

Lasers are very good for spectroscopy because they can be made to emit precise wavelengths. That lets them tell the difference between atoms and molecules with similar spectral lines. It also lets them detect very small quantities. In some experiments, lasers have found single atoms!

Laser spectroscopy has taught scientists many things about the structure of atoms and molecules. This research is so important that two people who pioneered the field, Nicolaas Bloembergen and Arthur L. Schawlow, shared the 1981 Nobel Prize in Physics for their work.

Earlier we saw how light causes chemical changes in photographic film or red dyes. Those aren't the only chemical changes that light can cause. By using spectroscopy, we can detect the presence of specific materials. If we put the pieces together, we can get some very powerful tools.

Suppose we want to separate two different types of atoms. One atom will absorb 500-nanometer light, but the other won't. And suppose that the 500-nanometer light will free an electron from the atom, giving it an electric charge. Then you can separate the two atoms by shining a 500-nanometer light on them and using a charged plate to collect the one that absorbs the light. The atoms that don't absorb the light will just sit there.

The example is simple, but the idea works. Department of Energy scientists have shown that lasers can make even more difficult separations, of different isotopes of uranium needed to fuel nuclear reactors. Isotopes are atoms with the same chemical properties but different numbers of neutrons in their nuclei. This makes them very hard to separate chemically. However, they absorb light at different wavelengths, so they can be separated by light.

Light also might help make chemistry work better. The reactions that produce complex molecules often are complicated, and many of them are not efficient—that is, they produce only a little of the desired material and a lot of waste. Light of just the right wavelength might help excite the molecules so they react in the desired way. Light might also help trigger certain chemical reactions in living cells or perform surgery on the genetic material in cells. Because light can be focused down to a very small spot, it might be able to select a specific spot on the gene to change.

Lasers and Nuclear Fusion

Another laser idea is being studied to help produce nuclear energy in a different way than today's reactors, by fusion. Fusion is the combination of light atomic nuclei together to make a larger nucleus. Stars like the sun get their energy from fusing hydrogen nuclei together to make helium. Because hydrogen is much more common on the earth than uranium, nuclear fusion could be an almost inexhaustible source of energy.

The problem is in taming fusion. Atomic nuclei normally repel each other strongly because they carry strong positive charges. They can only combine if they are moving fast and are pushed together tightly. That is, the fusion fuel must be very hot and dense. It is possible to make the right conditions in a hydrogen bomb, but that uncontrolled release of energy can only destroy. For more than thirty years scientists have been trying to find a way to confine fusion fuels so their energy can be extracted peacefully.

The leading approach has long been trying to hold the fusion fuel in a strong magnetic field that would keep it from cooling off. An alternative is to use an intense pulse of laser light to heat the fuel and squeeze it together. The fuel is packed into a tiny pellet, which is held in the middle of a special chamber. Then a very fast, very powerful pulse of laser light closes in from all sides. The light heats the fuel and squeezes it together for a very brief instant—but long enough for some of the hydrogen nuclei to fuse together and release energy.

Laser fusion won't produce electricity for many years, and some scientists think it may not be practical at all. However, it is one of the exciting possibilities of tomorrow's laser technology.

Light in Space

Optical technology has a future in space as well as on the ground. Light is already used in remote sensing from satellites. Scientists are working on laser systems that will be able to measure the concentrations of air pollutants and other materials from space. Compact optical computers may someday be put into satellites to help them recognize objects from space. NASA hopes to use fiber-optic communications in the space station it is planning, because optical fibers are much lighter than wires. And light may be used widely for communication in space.

Radio waves and microwaves now carry messages to and from satellites. Why change to light? Because a beam of light is much narrower. A basic law of physics says that the width of any beam of electromagnetic radiation depends on the wavelength and the size of the emitting area—a lens for optics or an antenna for radio waves. The longer the wavelength, the larger the beam. However, the larger the emitting area, the smaller the beam. Because radio waves are much longer than light, radio beams are much larger than light beams (unless the antenna is very large—and you can't put a huge antenna on a satellite).

That isn't a problem if you want to send messages from a satellite to a wide area. Suppose, however, you want to send messages between two satellites or to one specific spot on the ground, and you don't want anyone else to listen. Then you want a very narrow beam that will only go where you want it, not out to the sides. That's when light communication would be nice.

The Air Force and NASA have been working on laser systems to send messages between satellites, but light messages could go even further. Suppose you put a very powerful laser in space, with a very large mirror to focus its beam. Then it could send a very tightly focused beam far beyond the solar system. Such a laser might be able to send messages to beings living on a planet near another star.

Laser Propulsion

Huge lasers might have other uses in space travel. Some scientists think that a big enough laser could push a rocket in space.

How could laser light push a rocket? By heating a fuel at the base of the rocket, as shown in Figure 15–4. Suppose you built a huge laser under a launching pad and put a rocket on top of it. This rocket would not have ordinary rocket motors. Instead, its bottom would be ice or another material that the laser energy would heat. As the laser energy vaporized the material at the bottom of the rocket, the hot gases would push the rocket up, just as the hot gases from burning fuel push an ordinary rocket off the ground.

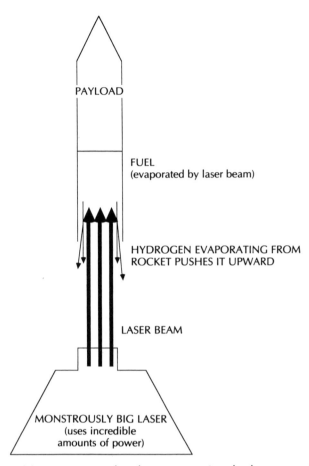

PAYLOAD

FUEL
(evaporated by laser beam)

HYDROGEN EVAPORATING FROM
ROCKET PUSHES IT UPWARD

LASER BEAM

MONSTROUSLY BIG LASER
(uses incredible
amounts of power)

FIGURE 15–4 *A laser could power a rocket by evaporating hydrogen or ice from its base, forming hot gas that would push it upward. The idea is intriguing, but it would require billions of watts of laser power to get a spacecraft into orbit from the ground.*

It takes a lot of energy to get a rocket off the ground, so you would need a very big laser. Some scientists have calculated that it would take billions of watts of laser power for half an hour. Such lasers cannot be built now, but smaller lasers might be used in space, because it takes much less energy to move a rocket from one orbit to another than it does to get it off the ground.

Why bother with laser propulsion when rockets can do the job now? Because laser-driven rockets could be much lighter and wouldn't need heavy motors and fuel tanks that consume energy to lift into space. The possibility is interesting, but you should understand that it is not going to be a reality in this century.

Visions for the Future

The science of optics may have its roots in ancient times, but as you have learned, it is far from stodgy. Although the roots go deep, the science of light has sprouted many new branches and is growing strong. The old parts can be as fascinating to explore as an old castle, and new additions are being built every day.

Looking at the future is like looking into fog; the farther away you look, the hazier the vision. We can already see how optics is changing the way we handle and communicate information. Fiber optics, optical disks, and optical computing all are coming, though we can't say when an optical fiber will come to your house. On the other hand, it is far too early to be sure that laser propulsion will work, let alone to predict that twenty-first century astronauts will ride to the stars on laser beams. New breakthroughs may appear to surprise and excite us, even if some of today's promising ideas don't work out. We cannot be sure of the future of light, but we know it will be exciting.

Index